Inversion of Magic

by
KateMarie Collins

Cover art image by:
Enrique Meseguer from Pixabay

Publisher's Note:

This is a work of fiction. All names,
characters, places, and events are the work
of the author's imagination.
Any resemblance to real persons, places, or
events is purely coincidental.

This title was originally released as 'Arine's
Sanctuary' in 2015.

For my children, two of the strongest people
I've had the privilege to know.

Prologue

The wagon bounced hard, jolting Arine awake. Rubbing her eyes, she looked around at the landscape. It was early morning, just past dawn. The forest was familiar in the dim light. Home wasn't far off. She stretched her arms towards the sky, willing the muscles in her back to wake with the rest of her.

She shifted a bit in the bed of the wagon. It was laden down with several boxes and bags, as well as a few other people from her village. Theos wasn't isolated, but it wasn't on a major caravan route either. Odd peddlers and such passed through often enough. Still, once or twice a year several of the tradesfolk banned together and made the run to Recor for supplies.

Arine moved aside the oilcloth covering the bundle next to her. The leather underneath it remained dry. It wasn't the rainy season, but she'd spent far too much of her mother's money on it to run the chance of spotting. Their shop was the only one for days in any direction to either have shoes made or repaired.

She bounced along with the wagon as the sun continued to climb over the horizon. Reaching a hand into her tunic, she felt the small bundle within. A smile crossed her face. Ian would love the colors she'd chosen. The pencils were a good quality, and far more expensive than she would normally have spent. There wasn't much she could give her brother that would make him as happy, though.

A smile crossed her face at the thought of her brother. While only two years younger than she was, he was small for fourteen. Ever since the accident that had claimed their father's life, Ian had lived in a world of his own creation. He could hear well enough, but rarely spoke to anyone besides Arine. She was the only one in Theos who could understand him. Not even their mother could. It seemed to Arine that their mother had given up trying to help Ian before she finished burying her husband.

For all his problems, Ian could draw beautifully. Sometimes she'd find him curled up at the hearth, charcoal and parchment on the floor next to him, where he'd fallen asleep while drawing the night before.

The creaking of the wagon seat alerted Arine, breaking her out of her reverie. Elaine looked down at her. "Last bend coming up, Arine. Wake the others."

The older woman turned back around, her long silvery braid swinging slightly.

Arine pushed a stray lock of her coppery hair out of her face before slowly waking the two others in the wagon with her. More had wanted to come on the run, eager to see the sights of Recor, but there wouldn't be enough room for them and their goods on the return trip home. Winter had been brutal, depleting stores below normal levels. Only four of them went this time, but the shopping list had been long.

The trees parted, giving way to the clearing where Theos sat. Arine took in the familiar houses and shops, dominated by the inn that took up the area behind the central well. Their wagon had been spotted already. Women poured forth from the buildings, voices calling out for help unloading, as they eagerly watched the wagon creep forward.

Arine kept silent, letting Elaine and the others answer the questions being put forth by everyone at once. She could barely keep the voices separate. Quickly, the wagon was emptied of all but the leather for Arine's mother and Elaine's own purchases.

Jumping down from the wagon, Arine reached in and pulled the leather bundle towards her. Her eyes scanned those still near the wagon, but Ian wasn't among them. *That's strange*, she thought. *Normally*

he's right here to carry the leathers for me.
Puzzled, she rearranged her own pack and
lifted the package from the wagon bed. At
least the shop wasn't a long walk away.

Struggling slightly to keep her hold
on the package, Arine found the latch to the
door. The door swung wide at her urging,
announcing her presence with a loud bang as
it hit the interior wall. Arine carefully
maneuvered past the tables and racks of
wares, grateful her mother had put off
rearranging the store until she returned.
Arine put the package on the back table with
a grunt. Leaning on it for a moment, she
called out, "Ma! Ian! I'm back!" When she
didn't hear a reply, Arine removed her pack
and placed it quietly on the floor behind the
table. The door to the work area was cracked
open. A small knot of fear formed in her
stomach. She moved to open the door,
looking inside the workroom.

Her mother sat at a workbench, her
back to Arine. The small fire, just big
enough to keep the room comfortable,
burned merrily in the fireplace. Tools were
placed on various surfaces, waiting to be
used. The chair Ian preferred sat empty.

"About time you got back, Arine.
Though Elaine said it might take a few more
days, given the lists of stuff everyone

wanted." Her voice rang in Arine's ears. The tone was wrong.

The older woman shifted, turning around to face Arine. Her dark hair was disheveled, strands fought against the tight braid she usually wore. "Did you get a decent amount of leather for me?"

Arine scanned the room. There was no sign of Ian. Not even a sketching. Those normally cluttered the corner of one of the tables. "Yes, Ma. I put them out on the table. You should be ok for a while." The fear in her stomach was growing. "Ma, where's Ian?"

The woman stood. Grabbing a thick cloth, she moved a steaming kettle away from the fire. Calmly, she poured herself a cup of tea before responding to Arine. "He's gone. Caravan came through, saw his drawings. Offered me good money to take him with them.` Said the Domines loved having artists in their houses."

"You sold him?" Aghast, Arine's voice shook with shock and fury.

"Not really. It's not like I could've gotten him a wife around here, Arine. He's not worth much to anyone. If the Domine likes having a mute fool for an artist, why shouldn't we get a chance to profit?" Reaching into the pocket of her trousers, the woman tossed a small pouch onto a table.

9

The heavy clink of coins echoed in the room. "That's your share. Go ahead. Take it. It'll go to your house, anyway, so might as well enjoy it now while you're young."

Arine stared at the pouch, her mind reeling. Ian had been sold. Like a piece of property. His only sin being born a boy. Slavery was illegal, but the Domines usually looked the other way when it came to boys.

"When did you do this?" Arine struggled to keep her voice neutral. However, if she could get information on when the caravan came through, she might be able to go after him. She kept her eyes on the pouch, unable to look at her mother.

"Two, maybe three days ago. The caravan didn't stay long. Lynn's stores in the inn were already fairly low. There were too many for her to feed beyond that." Her slurping of tea reached Arine's ears. "Pretty sure Lynn did some trading of her own. Saw a few new boys cleaning tables for her today. I'll bet you saw them as well. She would've sent them out to help unload Elaine's wagon."

Arine's mind worked frantically. Two- or three-days' head start! Very carefully, she reached out and took the pouch from the table. It was heavier than she expected. She'd need to find Bess first. Her friend could get all sorts of information from the new boys at the inn, and probably already had.

"I'm a bit thirsty from the trip, Ma. I'm going up to Lynn's to have a drink or two, recoup a bit. Don't wait up." Keeping a tight rein on her anger, Arine darted from the shop before anyone could stop her.

* * *

Two days later, Arine sat in an inn in some town. She'd lost track of names, of what direction she'd gone, searching for the caravan that now owned her brother. And of how much ale she'd had.

"This seat taken?" A voice, barely above a whisper, asked. Before Arine could raise her head to reply, the speaker pulled out a chair and sat down.

"You ready to listen to options, or are you still wanting to wallow in grief?" the voice asked.

Looking up, she took in the speaker. Dark hair pulled back in a braid, brown eyes that saw everything. The hilt of a sword peeking up past her ear. "What options?" she croaked; her voice raw from the alcohol.

"My mistress tasked me with seeking out those who had lost much, those who would do anything to regain what was taken from them. I've been following you since you left Theos. Heard you're searching for your brother." The young woman leaned in across the table. "She can train you, my mistress. Teach you how to save other boys from a fate like Ian's. And, one day, may be able to find him for you."

Arine shook her head, trying to take in her words. "And in return?"

The woman sat back in her chair. "Nothing. Mistress Bryn does not command loyalty, but earns it. The only question that remains is if you're willing to follow me."

"Follow you where?"

"To Sanctuary."

Chapter One

Arine maneuvered into the nook between chimneys as the clouds moved away from the moons, lighting both the street and the rooftops. Cel and Jos were full tonight, making her task more difficult. She whispered a silent prayer to Cinphire, more in desperation than any real hope that the Goddess would hear, then took a quick survey of the path in front of her. *May as well make use of the light*, she thought with a sigh.

Her Mistress told her this wasn't going to be easy, which was why Arine had been selected in the first place. Small and agile, she was perfect to leap across the red-tiled rooftops undetected. The hardest part thus far turned out to be getting from the tree, over the walls and into the city. Getting back out would depend on the agility of the one she was sent to fetch.

Clouds darted across the twin moons again. Seizing the opportunity, Arine ran silently across the rooftops. The slight slope of the roof tiles kept her from getting complacent even as she closed the distance between her hiding place and her destination. Huddled between chimneys again, absently tucking a stray strand of copper hair back under her hat, Arine caught her breath. She poked her head out of the shadows long enough to verify her position. The target's balcony loomed below her.

She lowered herself from the rooftop to the balcony's edge, keeping to the shadows as the dim glow of candlelight still illuminated the room. She needed to be careful now. It would be easier if he came along willingly, but she wasn't above knocking him unconscious and carrying him out.

Her senses spread out to the room. The sound of footsteps treading softly away from the window betrayed him. With another quick glance to check for watchers, she sidled up to the knob on the balcony door. A swift twist of her wrist opened it and before anyone could spot her, Arine disappeared into shadows within the room, easing the door closed behind her.

Her eyes quickly adjusted to the change in light as she hid behind the heavy drapery. The information about this man had been sketchy at best. Taking time to study one's prey before alerting them to her presence remained the primary reason she succeeded when so many others failed.

"I know you're there, behind the curtain." His voice carried softly across the room. He stopped in front of a small table, his back to her.

Arine emerged from behind the curtain, careful not to allow her expression to betray her surprise. "I've been sent to give you an alternative."

"An alternative? To tomorrow? You obviously don't know my mother." He slowly turned to face her. "If she says I'm to marry, I'm to marry."

"My Mistress sent me to offer you Sanctuary." She trod silently across the intervening space, her feet moving more slowly than her heart. Gods, but he was good-looking! Her Mistress didn't tell her that. Tall and lean, Cavon bore the likeness of his mother. Blonde hair curled slightly at the nape of his neck, blue eyes betraying intelligence. Younger than Arine by at least five years, he was built well for his age. At eighteen, he was barely old enough to be married off.

"Sanctuary? That's a dream. It's the duty of a son to marry for the advancement of the family." Cavon's deep voice cracked slightly.

"Yet it is not your desire, is it? You would stay here, marry the likes of Domine Elsa, and live your life as nothing more than a stud? Be trotted out all dressed up on special occasions? Be given as a treat to those who please her?" Try as she might, Arine couldn't keep the disgust from her voice. "My Mistress hands you the opportunity of freedom." She stopped in front of him, close enough to smell the perfumed oils from a bath.

She watched his face intently, waiting for him to make his decision. She knew how he would decide. The sigh finally escaped him; his head dropped in submission.

Arine spoke before he could change his mind. "We must move now. Get a dark cloak and some good shoes. It's cold tonight." Her hand grasped him firmly on the upper arm, propelling him to action. "Take nothing else. We don't have time for sentimental items." She slid up to the balcony door again, surveying the nearby homes for potential witnesses.

A quick glance over her shoulder told her he was ready. With an imperious gesture, she motioned him to her side. "We go out and up, quickly. Stay close to me at all times. The moons are full tonight, so keep to the shadows." Without a backward glance, she opened the door and climbed onto the roof in one fluid motion, then reached down to help him before he cleared the door.

Her eyes rolled skyward with the clatter he made as he followed her. None in the Moreja Sisterhood would be allowed to walk for a week if they made such noise! At least Cinphire had heard her prayer and the moons remained hidden behind the clouds.

It seemed like hours before the city walls emerged from the shadows. Arine glanced to each side, tracking the movement of the watch. They were both walking away from them. The narrow walkway along the top of the wall was worn smooth from their patrols. "We have to move fast here," she whispered to Cavon. "We cross the wall, climb into that tree over there," she gestured with her hand to a massive oak tree. "Once we're in the tree, move as quickly and quietly down as possible." Concern crossed his face. "What's wrong?" she asked him urgently.

"I've never climbed a tree. It looks dangerous." Cavon swallowed hard.

Oh, great, she thought silently. *He's been coddled!* Inhaling deeply, she tried to keep the annoyance from her voice. "It's like going down a flight of very crazy stairs. The steps are uneven, and some won't hold your entire weight. Think of it as a test of balance." His eyes brightened at her words. "Stay behind me, step where I step, and you should be fine." A quick glance reassured her of the guards' position. She reached out and grabbed his hand before she sprinted across the wall, dragging him behind her.

The tree proved more difficult than she feared for Cavon. He tried to stop every third branch, fascinated by some insect crawling near his hand or some other nonsense. "Move, damn you!" she hissed through clenched teeth. "If we get caught, Domine Elsa will be the least of your worries!" Shock flashed across his face, followed by understanding.

Arine lowered herself onto the lowest limb. Her hands gripped it firmly, giving herself time to adjust her balance before dropping to the ground. Her hand shot to the dagger at her waist, her ears alert for the sound of footsteps. A loud thump behind her caused her to spin on her heels. One of her daggers practically flew from the sheath at her side, ready to throw. She took in the sight of Cavon, sitting on the ground where he'd fallen from the tree.

He looked up at her, eyes wide. Slamming the dagger home again, she refrained from chastising him. The road to Sanctuary was long enough for that sort of education.

Reaching out a hand, she pulled him up off the ground. "We run first, then walk

when I decide it's safe to do so. Keep up."
She didn't wait for a response.

Chapter Two

The rain slid inside the neck of her tunic, a never-ending ribbon of cold that trickled down to the small of her back. The recent storm was a mild one. The larger drops falling from the trees truly irritated her, and the litany of complaints from her companion did nothing to improve her already sour mood.

"I really think we should be using the road," Cavon's whiny tone grated against her very raw nerves. "The mud is slippery and making it hard for me to keep my balance. We'd stay cleaner if we used the road."

Arine halted mid-step. Closing her eyes, she tried to gather at least some measure of calm. Then again, her Mistress never said she had to keep him talking. Tempting as it was to just knock him unconscious and carry him, she knew it would take too long. Absently, she pushed a wet strand of hair from her face as she turned to face him. He really wasn't more than an inch or two taller than her.

"Domine Elsa is looking for you by now. If your mother wants to keep her position and head, she's looking too, which means the road is going to be full of patrols, mercenaries and bounty hunters. Travel through the forest is much safer and faster."

Arine paused; the look in his eyes seemed almost amused. Before she could question him, it changed. His focus switched, as though he was looking past her instead of at her.

Instinct kicked in. Deftly, she dropped to a crouch and swept her leg around. She felt the leg of her attacker buckle before she saw her fall.

Arine leapt back to her feet, her hand drawing the dagger free of its sheath. Two more opponents rushed in as Arine's attacker got off the ground. "Leave the boy and go, Moreja. The Domine has no quarrel with you. Return what is rightfully hers and she will guarantee you passage." The woman Arine had kicked spoke evenly.

Arine snorted. "Guarantee me passage to her dungeon is all. The boy has been summoned by my mistress. He belongs to no one." Without warning, Arine lunged at the leader of the band. Her dagger left a mark on the woman's arm as Arine danced out of reach of the counterstrike.

The two women circled each other, daggers poised. From the corner of her eye, Arine could see the other two slowly moving in on Cavon. There was no fear on his face, and he'd found a broken branch to use as a weapon.

Arine's opponent lunged at her and she pushed all thoughts of Cavon from her head. The other woman had skill -- Arine had to give her credit. Knife fights were normally over before they began, but outside of her first strike, neither had been able to land a blow for several minutes. Her opening came when the woman glanced toward her companions, taking her eyes off of Arine just long enough for her to go in for the kill. A shot of pain that ran along her ribcage as she backed away from the falling body told Arine her opponent had marked her after all. Absently pressing a hand to her side, she spun to assist Cavon.

He stood silent, the cudgel hanging at his side. Two women lay on the ground in front of him. From the blood pooling beneath their heads, Arine knew they were dead.

"We need to keep moving." Arine's breathing was labored. "There will be more." Absently, she moved her hand from the cut on her side. Something didn't feel right. Her arm felt leaden as she raised her hand to her nose and took a whiff. The unmistakably sweet scent of cargrada assaulted her nose. She raised her head and looked at Cavon. The forest spun around him. Blackness engulfed her.

Fire ravaged her as the fever from the poison attacked. Vaguely, she knew she was moving. To where, she no longer cared. She sank back into darkness.

The next thing to she registered was the hard surface on which she lay. The recognition that it was stone, or at least very hard dirt, slowly penetrated the fog in her brain. The pop and crackle of a small fire pierced her consciousness. Slowly, she opened her eyes enough to see her surroundings.

She was in a cave of some kind, and a small fire burned nearby. She could hear someone moving about, but they were outside her line of vision. Whoever it was, they were trying not to wake her. She kept very still. Until she knew who was there, she didn't need them knowing she was awake.

A pair of legs came into her view. The figure crouched in front of the fire. With some relief, she realized it was Cavon.

"Where are we?" she asked quietly.

Her voice startled him enough that he almost lost his balance. "A cave, not far from where we were attacked. I thought it best to bring you here." There was something different about his tone of voice. Fear? Perhaps sadness?

Gingerly, she tried to put some weight on her arms to sit up. Cavon stood not far off, his back to her. Curiosity took hold as she carefully felt for the wound that should have killed her. No bandage. She twisted a bit to get a good look. The tear in her shirt remained. The skin underneath, however, was clean and uncut.

A vision tugged at the edge of her mind. *Cavon sat near her; a strange glow emanated from his hands. The fever from the poison slowly being eaten away by cold tendrils, a sensation she'd never felt before.* Now she looked at him. He kept his back to her.

"What did you do, Cavon? I should be dead." Her voice was even, infused with a slight hint of command. She kept her eyes on him as he turned around, leaning against the far wall. Slowly, he slid down the wall and slumped onto the floor. He refused to look at her. Fear was evident across his face. "I don't know," he whispered. Arine could hear the wavering in his voice. Whatever he'd done, it scared him.

She studied him for a few minutes, her blue eyes intent. The sooner she got him to Sanctuary and her mistress the better. "How many days have we been here?" she asked. Whatever secret he carried wasn't for her to discover.

Cavon raised his head, his brow furrowed in thought. "One, maybe two. I thought it best to set camp deep within the cave. Less likely the glow from the fire would be seen from the outside."

Arine nodded, making a mental note about the passage of time. "We need to get moving. Sanctuary's not much farther, another day or two of travel." She paused, shifting her legs so she could try to stand. "I don't suppose we still have any food or water?" Her stomach felt empty as a cauldron.

He reached over and began to rummage through her pack. "There's still some in here," he replied. "I figured you'd be hungry when you woke up." He took out a small packet and handed it to her. "There's a small stream running just outside the cave. I've been able to keep the water stores up." He twisted a bit to grab a bulging water skin.

Opening the packet, Arine resisted the urge to devour the dried meat and cheese. Deliberately, she took small pieces as she spoke. "Why the disguise, Cavon? Why hide who you are, your intelligence?"

He opened his mouth to protest, but abandoned the idea with the knowing look she gave him. He picked at his own meal. "It seemed safer. I was told as long as I can remember that I had to marry Domine Elsa.

And that she didn't like her men too smart. My entire childhood was geared to making me into the kind of man she'd be happy with. I tried, once, to question my lessons. Mother was furious. She told me I wasn't to question anything. I had no future unless I married the Domine, and she wanted me educated only in certain subjects." He shifted his legs a bit. "I still learned things I wasn't supposed to. I just stopped questioning the rest of it." A small grin split his face. "And I got very good at hiding both my books and intelligence."

Arine chewed on a piece of dried meat, her mind busy re-evaluating him. "I don't think you need to hide anymore, Cavon. I'd rather know you could defend yourself than have you complain about a sliver in your finger. Sanctuary's someplace you can relax and let that part of yourself come out. It will be better for both of us if you dropped the act." She chuckled. "You really don't want to know how close I was to knocking you unconscious just to get you to stop whining."

He laughed. "No, probably not." Arine felt the tension in the cave shift. His guard dropped slightly, replaced by a small measure of trust in her.

Arine started to stand up, anxious to test her legs. Cavon darted across the small space between them to help, but she waved him off. "If I can't stand alone, I won't be able to walk alone and time is running out. The longer it takes us to get to Sanctuary, the more of Domine Elsa's minions we'll have to avoid." A wave of dizziness threatened to overtake her, but she held fast against it. There was more strength in her than should have been after being poisoned. *I shouldn't even be alive*, she thought, *let alone standing*. Questions bounced about in her head, screaming for answers. Resolutely, she pushed them away. There was time for that when she was back in Sanctuary.

No rain met them when they emerged from the cave. Bright sunshine filtered through the thick forest. Steam rose from leaves as the remaining water evaporated. Squinting, Arine looked up and took note of the sun's position. It was still early morning.

"Up for a long day?" She looked over at Cavon. An expression of puzzlement crossed his chiseled features. "If we keep a good pace," she explained, "we should be in Sanctuary tonight." Taking his nod as assent, she led him away from the cave.

Hours later, the forest began to thin out. Ahead, through the trees, a massive peak loomed. Sheer rock sides gleamed from the recent rains. Arine stopped dead at the edge of the wood. Motioning for Cavon to be silent, she scrutinized the surrounding tree line.

"I don't see anyone, but that doesn't mean they aren't there. Domine Elsa wants to know where Sanctuary is more than anything. When we move out, stay with me. There won't be time for explanations. They will open the door for us only if we can get in and they can close it again before it's discovered." She turned her head towards the tor briefly before continuing. "They already know we're coming and will be ready for us."

Without further explanation, Arine grabbed Cavon's hand and pulled him forward as she crept the remaining few feet to the edge of the forest. The tunnel was only fifty feet away, but if someone was watching them, they both could be dead before reaching it. "Now!" she whispered as she launched into a dead run toward the tor.

A startled cry of alarm from the woods to her left reached her ears. She was right--they were watching the perimeter for Moreja returning to Sanctuary. Forty feet to go. She heard Cavon running hard behind her. The first arrow came at them with thirty feet to go. Twenty feet. More arrows rained down towards them. Quickly adjusting their course, she glanced over her shoulder long enough to make sure Cavon kept pace with her. Ten more feet. The tunnel mouth gaped in welcome. Their attackers screamed out for foot pursuit. Arine drew up short at the entrance to the tunnel, motioning Cavon through. Diving in behind him, she grabbed at his hand as she darted past him. "Stay with me now. Don't ask questions, just move when I tell you to." Timing now was critical. They needed to reach the door quickly.

The darkness in the tunnel didn't hamper Arine a bit as her familiarity with the passage told her where she was. Cavon stumbled here and there, doing his best to run in the dark. She rounded another bend, stopping quickly. Reaching back and grabbing him by the arm, she shoved him toward a gaping hole in the rock. She followed behind him as the stone door closed seamlessly behind her.

"You're late," a voice gently teased.

Arine turned to the source of the voice. "We ran into some problems."

A torch flared to life. Several women stood nearby, the mechanism to open and close the stone door visible behind them. "Is this the boy?" the one with the torch asked.

"Of course it is, Mestra. I don't make mistakes." Arine put her hands to her knees as she caught her breath.

Mestra laughed. "You're out of shape, Arine. You need to spend time working on that."

"I can still outrun arrows, and that's what counts." Straightening a bit, she nodded at the group. "Who does she want to see first? Me or him?"

"You. We've got a room ready for him. She wants to hear what went on from you before talking to him." Arine stepped up next to Mestra, motioning Cavon to walk behind them.

Arine walked calmly with Mestra, keeping up a litany of small talk. Nothing more would be said about Cavon until Mistress Bryn decided to share with the rest of them. They walked up a tunnel, keeping an even pace. All the women had made the same run she'd just made several times, and knew how exhausting it could be. None of them rushed up the tunnel.

Almost imperceptibly, the dim light in the tunnel began to increase and the roar of falling water reached Arine's ears. Smiling slightly, her heart lightened with the knowledge that she was so close to home. The tunnel bent one more time, opening up to reveal the hidden city below.

Arine turned around to face Cavon. "Welcome to Sanctuary," she said quietly.

Reaching out and taking him by the arm, she pulled him forward.

Chapter Three

The waterfall dropped into a partially hidden lake, churning the calm blue waters into a white torrent. A portion of the tor had broken off eons ago, letting sunlight shine down on small fields overflowing with crops. Shaded by what remained of the towering rock, row after row of neatly laid out buildings sat nestled in the shadows. Hundreds of people bustled about the cobblestone paths. Arine stayed back, letting Cavon take it all in.

After a minute or two, she broke the silence. "I need to report to my Mistress. Go with these women and they'll take you someplace you can rest and clean up."

Anxiety crossed his face.

"Don't worry, Cavon. All will be well," she reassured him. Turning on her heel, Arine began her descent down to the city below.

She strode purposefully through the busy streets, acknowledging the occasional greeting with a nod. Few ever tried to stop her. They knew what she had to do when she returned.

"About time you got back." The snide voice stopped Arine in midstep.

Whirling, she leveled a withering gaze at the man who spoke. "My comings and goings are of no concern to you, James, or the one you serve." Her blue eyes, filled with contempt, locked with black ones. A hint of fear showed on his face as she took a step closer. "Unless you care to explain to Mistress Bryn why you felt it necessary that I report to you before her, I suggest you crawl back into whatever hole Talia found you in and waylay me no more." Her tone was quiet, but firm.

She watched him swallow hard as he struggled to regain his composure. His hand shook slightly as he pushed back his stringy brown hair. "The Lady Talia suggests you watch yourself, Lady Arine. You won't hold your place as Mistress Bryn's favorite for long."

Snorting in disgust, Arine gave James a withering look. "Tell your Lady that I keep my position because I do my job better than she does. If she'd do as she was told and not try to collect a stable for herself, I might be concerned." Before James could reply, she turned and continued down the street.

Her destination finally emerged as she rounded a corner. She pulled on the bell rope harder than normal; irritation at James' brash manner made her want to spit. Judging from the startled expression of the woman who opened the door, she hadn't concealed it well.

The familiar space calmed her as she followed the woman toward Mistress Bryn's inner office. The plaster walls were decorated with an eclectic collection of paintings, some better than others. Oddly matched furniture sat in various rooms, all functional if not aesthetically pleasing. Mistress Bryn was often given gifts by those who had come to Sanctuary after learning a trade. While not always tasteful, she accepted them all with a graciousness that made the maker feel special.

The corridor ended at a pair of double doors. The fabric covering the panels had faded over the years, becoming threadbare in places. Yet it remained, as it was another gift from a new arrival. Arine shoved the encounter with James from her mind and smiled at the memory of how Mistress Bryn accepted her gift with glee. It was not long after that day, however, that the weaver told Arine she was to learn a completely different art.

She rapped lightly on the door, framing her report in her mind.

"Come in, Arine," Mistress Bryn's melodic voice beckoned her.

Placing a slender hand on the brass handle, she pressed downward with a slight amount of force. The handle had a tendency to stick. The door shuddered slightly before giving her admittance.

Mistress Bryn sat at her desk; her blonde head bent over a sheaf of paper. Arine knew to wait for her to finish. Interruptions were a pet peeve in this office. Silently, she slid into a chair across from the ornately carved wood desk and waited.

"You are late. I expected you a day or two ago." Mistress Bryn kept writing.

"It was unavoidable. Some hunters caught up with us. We … had to take a few days to recover." Arine shifted uncomfortably in her chair.

"Was Cavon injured?" The sound of her quill on the paper echoed in the still room.

"No, he wasn't." Unable to stay still, Arine rose nervously. Crossing the room, she stared out of a window to a small courtyard garden below.

The writing stopped. She could feel Mistress Bryn's green eyes on her as she shifted in her chair.

"You were? That does not happen often. The hunters you encountered were well-trained?"

Arine nodded silently from her place at the window. Drawing in a deep breath, she replied, "They had access to cargrada. Their blades were laced with it."

Footsteps crossed the carpeted floor. A gentle hand touched hers, urging her to sit on a small couch. Sinking into the soft cushions, Arine struggled to regroup. She looked at the concerned face across from her. Mistress Bryn sat next to her, patiently waiting for Arine to continue.

"One of them got lucky. A dagger thrust to my side that was just a shade too fast for me to parry. I woke up a day or so later in a cave. Cavon found it, brought me there." She paused, unsure of what Mistress Bryn would believe.

"They couldn't have been using cargrada, Arine. You'd be dead if they had."

Arine met her eyes, and Mistress Bryn sat back, her face unreadable. "What else happened, Arine? Even if you are uncertain, I need to know." Her voice carried a tone of command that Arine knew better than to resist.

Drawing in a deep breath, she plunged into retelling her sketchy memories of the cave, of Cavon's reaction when she woke up. Mistress Bryn listened in silence. Her story complete, Arine raised her face, expecting to be told she imagined it.

To her surprise, Mistress Bryn sat still. Small creases in her forehead appeared like they always did when she was deep in thought. "How much do you know of the old tales, Arine?" Her voice remained light, but there was a serious undertone.

"The same as everyone else. We're all taught them as part of our learning. That some men once wielded magic, those who didn't controlled those who did. How the Great War almost killed both our people and the land. That those who were left, the first Domines, seized power so that the warmongering of men could never happen again. The mages died out. No one was willing to admit to using magic; it was banned as a consideration in a dowry. The lineages of power were broken." She spoke evenly. The lecture regarding the history of the Great War was one of the more boring things she'd ever sat through, and the scariest. Magic led to death.

An almost oppressive silence hung in the room. Mistress Bryn's uneven breath made Arine's ears perk up. "And if I told you that Cavon was descended from the lineage of one of the greatest mages, and that magic had saved your life, would it change how you saw him?" The look in Mistress Bryn's eyes sent a cold shiver down Arine's spine.

She looked away, momentarily stunned. She recited in a sing song voice, "The Law is absolute. Any boy found with the ability to wield magic is to be put to death. The Domines will not allow ...". Her voice trailed off. Cavon? A mage? Her hand absently moved to where her wound had been. The skin felt cool beneath her fingers.

"Not all magic is evil, Arine. The reason Domine Elsa wants him is to mingle her bloodline with his. She wants mages she can control." Arine closed her eyes and she shuddered with the thought of what could happen if that came to pass.

"This is why you had me fetch him? To keep him from her? Why not just have me kill him?"

"Would you have Logan executed as well?" Arine whipped her head around, fear knotting her stomach. Not her Logan! He couldn't be one of them!

"We didn't know until yesterday, Arine, and neither did he. There was a minor incident, and he reacted without thought. It took me the better part of an hour to calm him down. He was ready to end his own life because of it."

Arine slumped forward, burying her head in her hands. She'd fetched Logan from another town about three years ago. Less than a year later, she'd allowed him to share her bed. It was unclear to both of them when they decided he should live with her. An image of his lean face, brown hair framing ice blue eyes, formed in her mind. His was the face she wanted to see when she came back from Mistress Bryn's errands.

"He is waiting for you at your home, Arine. Go there; see for yourself he has not become the monster your instructors told you he would be. I need to talk with Cavon." The note of dismissal was impossible for her to ignore. Slowly, she rose from the couch and exited the room. It would be a long time before she would sleep.

Chapter Four

Dark shadows filled the streets as Arine made her way toward home, the flickering candles in the lamps offering some meager light. She knew this street well, better than the one leading to Mistress Bryn's house. She'd been walking it since the day she first came to live here.

The alley was narrow, but uncluttered. Many of her neighbors came home late like she did. They all kept it clean. Nothing for them to trip over in the dark, or for others to hide behind. Life wasn't perfect here in Sanctuary, but it was better than most places.

The light from the sconce near her door guttered in the slight breeze, fighting the impulse to go out. Smiling, Arine felt herself relax a bit. Logan always kept it lit when she wasn't around. It was his way of welcoming her home.

Slipping silently through the door, she lowered her pack and cloak to the tile floor. Easing the door shut, she moved the latch slowly to minimize the noise it would make as it clicked home. The tan walls reflected the meager light that shone from the main living area. She sat down on the small bench nearby, taking her time in removing her leather boots. Dried mud dropped in flaky chunks onto the floor. She'd clean it up later. Silently, she crept towards the light. No noise reached Arine's ear. It was late though. He might be asleep. Still, she remained cautious. Meeting James on the street wasn't an accident and she knew it. Talia was growing bolder; the jealousy she had for Arine's position becoming clear to everyone among the Moreja.

The simply furnished room held only one person. Logan lay on the couch, eyes closed as if asleep. A strand of brown hair had come loose from the tie he normally kept it secured in, falling across the bridge of his nose. On silent feet, she crossed the room and removed a blanket from a chest he'd left open. Trying not to rouse him, she spread it across his lean frame.

"You're late." Logan's deep voice held no accusations.

Settling down to sit near his head on the floor, Arine smiled briefly. "It couldn't be helped."

She watched him shift slightly, resisting the urge to move the stray lock of hair. "One of these days I'll actually get Mistress Bryn to let you come home before reporting." He opened his eyes and looked at her.

Arine finally gave in and reached out to brush aside the wayward lock. "You know that'll never happen. She likes to get her reports before small details are forgotten." She paused, choosing her words carefully. "I understand you had your own adventure while I was gone this time." She tried very hard to keep her tone neutral. Mistress Bryn's revelation that Logan had used magic still left her uneasy.

She watched him carefully as he rolled onto his back, looking at the ceiling instead of her. "I don't know how it happened, Arine. I was in the shop, preparing the wicking for the day's candles. Julia was in the back, working with the wax. I heard a crash and ran in. She stood there, pale. The kettle had fallen off the chain and pinned her against the wall. I didn't think. I just wanted to move the kettle before it crushed her legs. It came off the ground without me touching it. She moved away, and it crashed back to the ground. Next thing I knew, Mistress Bryn was there." He paused; a tear slowly trickled from his eye. "I don't want this, Arine. I don't want to be a monster."

She reached a hand toward him, frantically searching her brain for the right thing to say. A loud crash as the door flew open resounded in the room before she could utter a word. Arine bolted to her feet, her hands flying to the daggers at her side. She heard Logan standing up behind her.

Several women, and a few men, filled the room. All were armed, the unmistakable green and gold badge of Talia's personal guard present on each of their tunics. Arine didn't lower her weapons, choosing to stand ready against the intruders.

Talia sashayed in, her black hair swinging in rhythm with her steps. James skulked in behind her, shadowing her every step. Arine watched warily as she took her time surveying the room.

"Get out of my house, Talia," Arine growled through clenched teeth.

Talia smiled coldly. "No, I don't think I will. Not for a very long while. I rather like it. I'll have to redo the décor, you understand. Just not my taste at all."

"You've got that hovel you call a home. Mine's occupied."

"Not for long, Arine. You and that *thing*" -- she thrust her chin contemptuously toward Logan – "are under arrest. Please tell me you're planning on resisting. I'd be terribly disappointed if you came peacefully." Her black eyes were filled with contempt.

"What are the charges?" Arine demanded.

"Harboring a mage, and assisting Mistress Bryn in bringing another here." The disgust in her voice hit the cold lump in Arine's stomach like ice.

Arine quickly assessed the strength of the guards Talia had brought with her. She could easily dismiss James and one or two others as no match for her, but there were still too many for her to know she'd win any fight. Logan wouldn't be a help, either. He dealt with wax and candles all day, not weaponry. Reaching back, she found his hand and squeezed it reassuringly.

"I think I'll have to disappoint you today, Talia. If there's to be a fight, let it be before the Council. I answer to them, not you." Arine paused, putting every ounce of contempt she could muster into her voice. "The truth will come out, Talia, and I doubt I'll be on the losing side. You're nothing but an opportunistic wench. If you spent more time on your skills and less on plots, you might be worth notice." With that, she sheathed her daggers and allowed herself and Logan to be escorted from her home.

Chapter Five

Arine paced in her cell, her mind racing. She'd been thrown in here close to an hour ago while Logan was led to another cell. Her mind refused to think of what might be happening to him. Picking the lock would do her no good. She wasn't sure where to go, or who might hide her.

From the sounds that filtered down from the street above, there was chaos in Sanctuary. Snatches of conversation let her know Mistress Bryn had been arrested as well. Talia had organized this well, quickly arresting those she felt would stand against her. She couldn't arrest the Council, though. The laws that governed them all would be followed.

The sound of footsteps reached her ears, but she kept her back to the door. The door closed again with a hollow sound. Arine waited for the footsteps to recede before turning to see who now shared the cell with her.

Mistress Bryn stood near the wall of bars, her hands trying to smooth the front of her dress. Her disheveled hair and the slight tremor in her hands spoke volumes to Arine's trained eye. She wasn't as confident as she wanted Arine to believe.

45

Arine patiently waited for Mistress Bryn to finish calming herself.

"I take it they have Logan?" Bryn's voice was steady.

"Yes." Arine leaned against the wall, trying to keep her composure. "I haven't seen him for over an hour."

"She won't kill him, Arine. Not yet. I was able to gather some information before Cavon and I were taken. Talia plans on turning them over to Domine Elsa. She is more concerned with you and I than the men." She drew a deep breath. "I've known for some time that Talia was ambitious. I underestimated how far she would reach. I thought she only wanted to supplant your rank in the Moreja. I didn't know she wanted my office as well. For that, I apologize to you. I should have seen this coming."

"None needed. Talia's an opportunist. She would've jumped at the first chance to get rid of me. If she could get rid of you as well, that would be a bonus. But I can't help but think there's a flaw in her plan." Arine started pacing again, slower this time.

"You have something in mind, then?" Bryn's voice carried a bit of hope.

"I do. She can't kill any of us, not without the Council agreeing to it. And I doubt she'll dare to present her charges to them without all four of us. Therefore, she can't hand them over to Domine Elsa before the tribunal is convened. We need to present a reasonable argument that they will accept and show we broke no laws. Not Sanctuary laws, at least." Arine smiled slightly at the last. She and Bryn both knew she'd broken plenty of the Domine laws each time she went to fetch someone.

Bryn raised her head, leaning it against the gray stone behind her. "You'll have to present it, you know. We can't have Talia claiming prejudice against the Council. Any time a Council member comes before them in tribunal, another must speak for them."

"I know. Do you want to know how I will argue beforehand?"

Shaking her head, Bryn glanced out the cell. "No. There are too many unfriendly ears in here. Do what you must to keep yourself and the boys free. They *cannot* be given over to Domine Elsa, Arine! If she gets her hands on two mages, war will reach even here."

The sound of a door opening nearby grabbed Arine's attention. Two large women entered, dragging Logan's limp body between them. She could easily make out several large bruises on his face and arms, the color fading from red to purplish black already. A small trickle of blood flowed from the corner of his mouth. She grasped the bars of the cell as he was paraded past her. Her only consolation was the even movement of his chest. He was still alive. Arine watched intently as the guards deposited him in the cell to her left before walking away.

A hand gently touched her shoulder. Jumping slightly, she turned to meet Bryn's concerned look. Arine looked away, choosing to sit on the small cot in the cell.

"At least you know he's alive, Arine. Hurt, to be certain, but also alive and close enough to talk to you when he wakes up." Bryn's gentle voice reminded her all was not lost.

"They must've decided to work on Cavon next. I'm sure he'll be able to get through it. He proved rather resourceful on the way here." Arine tried to change the focus of the conversation.

"When he wasn't driving you mad with his whining?" Bryn chuckled. "He told me about that, you know. He wasn't certain he could trust you completely. You gave him the chance at freedom, but he didn't know if you would accept him if you knew what he could do."

Arine raised her head to look at Bryn. "What is he, exactly?"

Myriad emotions played across Bryn's gentle features. Arine watched in fascination as the blonde woman's face focused on some long-held memory. "He's a healer, Arine. What he did for you in that cave was only the second time he's harnessed his ability, but I'm very grateful he did so. It's also why Domine Elsa wants him so bad. With a healer like Cavon and a handler like Logan, she could wreak havoc on this world. Her thirst for power rivals that of the men from the histories."

"He's healed someone before, then?" Arine kept her voice neutral.

Bryn nodded. "I lived in a small village in lands ruled by Domine Erenda, Domine Elsa's mother. Cavon and my younger sister were playmates. One day, I was inside the house when I heard my sister screaming outside. I ran out and saw her sitting on the ground, her foot twisted at an angle that was painful to even look at. Cavon sat next to her, his hands over her ankle. Something that looked like lightning was running from his hands. Her foot straightened itself as if it had never been broken." She paused, looking off to the center of the cell block. "Before I could get to her, Domine Erenda was there. Cavon's

49

mother and mine stood behind her. They had all seen what happened, and the Domine ordered my mother to take me and my sister from the village that night, on pain of death. We were never to speak of what we saw. We heard rumors months later that a betrothal was sealed between Elsa and Cavon."

Arine studied Bryn carefully. "Why not send me before now? Why wait until just before he was to marry her?"

Bryn shrugged. "I wanted to make sure whoever I sent to fetch him would be able to bring him back in one piece." She took a deep breath. "I know what Elsa is capable of, Arine. She can't have the kind of power that Cavon and Logan are capable of."

Arine nodded. The information would prove helpful when she spoke to the Council. The exhaustion she'd been fighting off for hours now finally proved stronger than her will to remain awake. She curled up on the straw ticked mattress and hoped Logan would be awake the next time she opened her eyes.

Chapter Six

Arine walked beside Bryn, the echo of their boots resounding off the stone floor. The torches carried by the guards surrounding them left a trail of thick black smoke on the cold stone walls. Logan hadn't made those torches. His didn't give off that much smoke. She drew a shuddering breath, trying to regain her focus. She would soon be fighting for their lives. She had to keep distractions to a minimum.

A set of massive double doors came into view at last. The dark wood was intricately carved and polished to a mirror-like finish. The wood reflected the torchlight. The polished brass hinges reflected the torchlight back towards them.

The lead guard halted before them, placing the torches within the sconces set into the walls. Not a sound came through the thick wood, but Arine didn't expect any either. She had sat in on a few tribunals, been called in as a witness once or twice. The gallery rarely spoke out. The solemnity of the proceedings kept conversations to a whisper at most.

She knew what was happening in there. The Council members would be filing in, finding their seats. The women and men who sat upon it would be directly in front of them when the doors opened, their blue and green robes immaculate. One seat of the nine would be empty -- Bryn's seat. They both wore the clothing they had been arrested in, which suited Arine just fine. Her presentation would be better suited with Bryn out of the blue robe that marked her as the missing member.

Arine was met by a blast of cool air as the doors swung open away from her. Light from the Council chamber gradually replaced the torchlight. She glanced to her right, meeting Bryn's reassuring grin with a tight one of her own. Arine drew in a deep breath, steadying herself for the war she was about to wage.

The dark, polished wood of the gallery walls shimmered in the bright morning light that filtered through the windows. The tiled floor gleamed brilliantly as she and the others were escorted to a row of four chairs. A small podium stood in front of the chairs. To her left, Talia sneered from an identical dais. James sat in a chair behind her, his face barely concealing his mirth. Arine let her eyes travel through the gallery of witnesses, seeing many of her fellow Moreja. She locked eyes for a moment with her friend Mestra, drawing strength from the support she read in those green eyes. Arine rested her gaze at last upon the Council members seated in front of her, keeping her eyes on them as she took a seat. She refused to look at Bryn, Logan or Cavon. They weren't the ones she needed to convince of their innocence.

A single deep note of a large bell rang throughout the room, signaling the start of the proceedings. A tall, slender woman spoke. "Let the tribunal before this Council begin. Lady Talia, being that you are the accuser, you will speak of the charges. Who will speak for the accused?"

Arine rose smoothly. "I shall speak for those accused." With a nod from the moderator, she crossed the short distance to the podium on silent feet.

The moderator glanced to the Council, waiting for permission to continue. A woman Arine had met once or twice-- Mistress Gwen, she thought her name was-- made a small gesture with her hand. Looking back to Arine and Talia, the moderator said, "Lady Talia, what are the charges you would accuse these individuals of?"

"The men who sit with them I accuse of being mages. They have worked magic, which is forbidden by law. The women I accuse of willfully bringing them to Sanctuary and hiding the knowledge of their

53

magic from all, thus placing all within our boundaries in danger. The blonde man is the betrothed of a Domine, and to interfere with the desires of a Domine is a death sentence." Talia's voice rang hollow in Arine's ear.

"And what would you have done with them should they be found guilty?" The deep voice of one of the male Council members reverberated across the chamber.

Arine kept her eyes focused on the Council, refusing to look at Talia. What she would say was pivotal to how Arine would argue their side. "For the women, they should be stripped of all rank and privilege and made to labor in a way to benefit Sanctuary. The boys should be returned to Domine Elsa. One is her betrothed, after all. Let her determine their fate."

The moderator looked to Arine; her face impassive. "Lady Arine, how do you and your companions answer to these charges?"

Arine took a deep breath. "I find it most interesting that Lady Talia comes to you asking for this Council to uphold Domine law and break it at the same time. Sanctuary came into existence by a group of individuals who suffered under those edicts. They created their own laws to ensure the safety and security of not just those who first came here but to protect all who would follow. That is one reason the Moreja exist; to give those who would escape the thumb of dictatorship a way here. To give all who would come the opportunity to learn a trade and not be subject to a life decided by others. With that in mind, I think Lady Talia does all in Sanctuary a grave disservice by asking that we abide by Domine law."

She shifted a bit on one leg, taking the time to meet all the council members' eyes. "As to the charge of Logan and Cavon being mages, this is true. It was not known to either myself or Mistress Bryn that Logan possessed the ability until recently, when his quick actions saved the life of Julia in her candle shop. I did not know of Cavon's aptitude when I was sent to fetch him. I learned of it on our way here, when he saved my life. I can only say that it scared him to work magic. Mistress Bryn knew of Cavon, yes. Her motivation for bringing him here was to deny Domine Elsa of the chance to abuse his abilities.

"Sanctuary law states that all who seek us are welcome, provided they mean to do no harm. There is no provision for mages any more than there is for a woodworker or weaver. Shall we now turn away a talented individual in need of Sanctuary because we have enough scribes?

"Domine law states that all who are proven to work magic must be put to death. No exceptions. Yet Lady Talia would ask that you hand two such mages over to a Domine alive and healthy. Even give her the right to marry one of them, against his wishes, over putting him to death as their own law demands. This makes me wonder at not just Domine Elsa's motives, but Lady Talia's as well. Could she be assisting the Domine, thus putting all here at risk?"

Arine lowered her arms from the podium, signaling to the Council she was finished with her initial argument. She read the faces of the Council members closely, hoping to see if any might be now inclined to her side.

Mistress Gwen's voice carried across the chamber. "You make some interesting points, Lady Arine. Should we decide in the favor of your side, what would you consider fair penalty to Lady Talia?"

She finally dared a glance over to Talia. Talia's hands clenched the side of her podium so hard that her knuckles were white. It must have cost her every ounce of control she had not to interrupt Arine. "I seek no penalty. I would offer to the Council that I am willing to meet her in the Ring should the matter not be settled without a blood price." Talia's face went white at

Arine's words. Arine would beat her in a duel and they both knew it.

The moderator spoke again. "Let those who come before this tribunal remain. The Council will consider this matter." Opening a small door near the Council, she held it for the Council members as they filed out quietly.

Arine sat back down, letting out an explosive breath. A pat on the shoulder from Bryn helped to calm her. What happened next was out of her hands.

The bell rang again, far sooner than Arine had anticipated. She and the others rose to their feet as the Council filed back in.

"After review, we find that Lady Arine has truly quoted Sanctuary law. As none of our laws were broken, the charges are found to be baseless." Mistress Gwen paused, looking at both Arine and Talia. "The Council is willing to give you the opportunity to settle upon a blood price, as requested, and the Ring is being prepared now. All those in the matter other than the Lady Arine and Lady Talia are free to depart. Ladies, prepare yourselves. Your weapons await you in the Ring within the quarter hour." With that, the Council once again rose and filed out of the room.

Arine turned her attention to Mistress Bryn. "Take them someplace safe, if you would. Logan's wounds will need to be tended to. I won't be long."

Mistress Bryn stood, every inch the Council member once again. "Be careful, Arine. I know precautions are in place to keep her from being less than honorable, but she will still try."

Arine snorted. "She can try all she wants. Doesn't mean it'll work." Throwing a quick reassuring glance past Mistress Bryn to Logan, she darted off towards the lawn where the Ring would be placed.

The appointed time for the duel arrived. Talia didn't.

Chapter Seven

The sound of the blacksmith's hammer rang through the open window and into Mistress Bryn's office. Logan wasn't at the candle shop today. He and Cavon were closeted with some of the older men, researching how they might control their abilities. Talia was long gone. A search of her home had led to the discovery of letters, proof of her collusion with Domine Elsa. Had things gone Talia's way, the mechanism that kept them safe and hidden would have been destroyed. Domine Elsa would have walked in with an army at her back, and Sanctuary would've been leveled.

A rustling of papers at the desk behind her was enough to let Arine know that she had been noticed. Mistress Bryn's calm voice cut across the silence in the room.

"Arine, I have someone I need you to fetch for me."

* * *

Arine all but ran through the streets once Mistress Bryn gave her the name of who she was to bring back. Mestra was being given the details and would run lead on the assignment. She didn't like it, but Arine knew why it had to be so. Mestra knew enough of Arine to keep her from letting her emotions get the better of her.

Dodging around the last corner, she pushed the hood of her cloak away from her head as she made for the door halfway down the alley. There was a lit candle in the lantern above the door. *Good*, she thought, *he's home*.

"Logan!" Arine called out breathlessly as she sidled through the door. Her fingers were taking the cloak off before the latch clicked home behind her. She tossed the garment towards a vacant hook, not caring if it caught or not. "Logan!" Damn it, she couldn't keep the excitement out of her voice.

The smells and sounds of the house told her he was in the kitchen. Another voice caught her ear. Cavon must be eating with them again tonight. She darted into the kitchen, pulling up short in the doorway.

Logan was near the stove, stirring a pot of something. He turned and looked her way, concern all over his face. "Arine? What's wrong?" Wiping his hands carefully on a towel, he crossed the room to her.

Arine smiled. "Nothing. Nothing will ever be wrong again." She paused, taking Logan's hands into hers. "Mistress Bryn's sending me and Mestra out together. A joint retrieval." She took a deep breath before continuing. "She found him, Logan. She found Ian." Unable to control her joy, Arine leapt into Logan's arms with a laugh.

A cough brought her back to the room. Cavon sat at the table, puzzled. "Who is Ian?"

"Ian's my brother, Cavon. My mother sold him while I was away on a supply run over ten years ago, before I came to Sanctuary." She gave herself a moment to catch her breath. "I need to put my gear together. I'll tell you more at dinner." Turning, she started to leave.

"When do you leave, Arine?" Logan called out to her.

Arine turned her head briefly. "Tonight. There's a storm coming in. The extra clouds will make the night even darker." The excitement started to build in her once again as she headed towards the bedchamber.

Her pack was always out, ready to grab at a moment's notice. Mistress Bryn often got information that needed to be acted upon immediately. Some things, such as daggers, rope, and bandages, stayed in the pack constantly and were replenished as needed. Arine started throwing in some tunics when she noticed her hands trembling. Heavily, she sat on the edge of the bed as the truth began to really sink in.

61

This was why she accepted the offer to join the Sisterhood. The possibility of finding Ian, being able to bring him here to Sanctuary, drove her each time she went out. Every time she went on a retrieval, Arine would pray she arrived before it was too late. Her blue eyes caught the corner of a piece of paper jutting out from the chest of drawers. Rising, she crossed to the chest. She opened the drawer slightly before pulling the paper out. The rolled-up page was secured with a small scrap of ribbon. A tear rolled silently down her cheek as she untied the ribbon. With great care, Arine unrolled the page and looked at it.

Her younger self stared back at her. None of the cares she now shouldered were impressed down on that face. It was a face full of hope and excitement. Ian had drawn it while she was gone on the supply run for the village, and then left it for her when their mother sold him.

"I know you're there, Logan," she whispered. She wiped at the tracks left on her cheeks from the tears that had escaped, but didn't turn around.

She heard the door close and the even tread of his feet across the wooden floor. His arms encircled her waist. She leaned back, grateful for the extra strength. "Mestra's here," he told her quietly.

Arine took a deep breath, exhaling slowly. Her fingers absently traced the signature at the bottom of the portrait. "I've waited so long, Logan. What if he doesn't remember me?"

A deep chuckle rumbled from Logan. Arine could feel it through his body. "I may be a little biased, Arine, but you tend to stick in people's minds." She turned to face him. His face was alive with both love and excitement for her. "This is why you do what you do. To find boys like him, or me and Cavon even, and keep us from those who would use or abuse us. I can't say what his life has been like for the last ten years, but I doubt he forgot about his big sister." Arine buried her head in his chest for a moment, glad for his understanding. Perhaps now, once she had Ian home, she could put the ghosts of her past to rest at last and be able to put Logan before her job for a change.

Raising her head, Arine smiled up at Logan. "So, do I have time to eat or is Mestra already trying to push me out the door?"

He smiled down at her, his ice blue eyes filled with mirth. "You have time to eat. Though I think Mestra is as anxious to get on the road as you are. I'm not sure why

else she'd be here so early if she wasn't."
He turned, heading towards the door.

Arine knew why Mestra was here,
though she kept it to herself. Her friend had
fixed her eye on Cavon almost as soon as
they'd arrived in Sanctuary. She knew
Mestra well enough that she would wait for
Cavon to settle into his new life before
really pursuing him.

Quickly, she finished her
preparations and closed the pack tight
against the storm. Hefting it over her
shoulder, she left the room to rejoin the
others in the kitchen.

She dropped the pack on the floor
near the door. Mestra sat at the table,
listening to Logan give Cavon cooking
advice. The young man had been given a
small apartment but was in serious need of
learning how to take care of himself.

Arine slid into a seat at the table.
"So, where are we off to?" Try as she
might, she couldn't keep the curiosity out of
her voice.

Mestra paused, sipping at the mug of
steaming cider in front of her. Her green
eyes refused to meet Arine's blue ones.
Instead, she watched Cavon's back. "Later,
Arine. I'll tell you once we're on the road
tonight." She paused, her voice dropping to
a whisper. "Mistress Bryn has her reasons

for keeping you in the dark for a bit longer, Arine. If it wasn't for the fact that your presence might help us convince Ian to come with us, she would've left you here. She was very adamant about what you can be told, and when." She lowered her mug to the table, one finger absently tracing the rim. Looking up, Arine could see how hard it was for Mestra to keep secrets from her. "There are reasons, Arine. Very good reasons. Or things would not be as they are. I do not do this to cause you pain." Arine nodded. It was one of the things Mistress Bryn had spoken of her often. She was so emotionally invested in finding Ian that it could easily blind her to dangers. That was something that could get her or others killed in her line of work.

Logan and Cavon put steaming bowls of stew in front of her and Mestra, followed by a platter of dark bread in the center of the table. Arine waited for them to sit as well before starting her own meal. The group ate in silence, each lost in thought.

As the dishes were being cleared, Mestra placed a hand on Arine's shoulder and nodded towards the door. Nodding once in understanding, Arine quietly slipped out of her chair. The pair moved towards the front door. Not a word was said as they put their packs on, followed by heavy cloaks. Mestra slipped out the door first. Arine paused, glancing back at the kitchen with a small pang of guilt. She'd never snuck out like this, not since she'd met Logan. There had always been some kind of farewell between them. But she wasn't the lead on this retrieval. She turned towards the door and sidled through, closing it silently behind her.

Chapter Eight

The rain was warm for this time of year, which helped Arine's mood. Warm rain was infinitely better in her mind than a cold rain. The dark night helped keep their visibility down. Arine deftly darted behind Mestra, following in her steps as much as possible so any trackers only thought there was one instead of two.

As soon as they'd left Sanctuary, Mestra headed to the south. That was towards Domine Grace's lands. And the seaports. Arine had never seen the ocean, but heard tales of the vast body of water, the women who sailed it, and of lands on the other side. Mestra was originally from one of those seaports. Having her as lead made sense to Arine, though she still wanted to know everything that Mestra knew about Ian.

Mestra kept up a quick pace, which made Arine keep focused on her footing over the questions filling her mind. What if Ian didn't recognize her? Or her him? Would he come willingly with her? And, what had he become over the last ten years?

Dawn began to break before Mestra stopped. "There's a cave up ahead. We'll take a rest in there. Few travel this way, and

the cave is deep. We won't be disturbed."
The woman looked Arine in the face. "You
will get some information then, Arine. Our
destination and what I was told of Ian in
order to find him. But we have to get there
first." Arine nodded, anxious now to reach
the cave. Mestra's braided brown hair
swung almost violently as she turned and
darted forward again. Arine's own coppery
braid followed suit as she chased after
Mestra.

The cave was perfect. Arine
followed Mestra into the depths of the
cavern. They were deep inside before
Mestra lit a torch. The tunnel twisted
several more times before Mestra found a
smaller tunnel leading to the left. "We'll go
this way," Mestra said calmly. "There's a
small room off of here that I've used several
times. Most people don't come this deep.
Those who do tend to ignore this passage. It
gets pretty narrow right before the room, so
we'll have to pass the packs through by
hand." Arine shrugged her pack off, and
then took the torch so Mestra could do the
same. She handed the torch back, nodding
her readiness.

Following the glow of the torch,
Arine moved carefully through the
passageway. Suddenly, the walls closed in
towards each other. Mestra stopped before a

very narrow slit in the wall. Arine's small frame would fit easily, though it would be a tight squeeze for a man. Mestra dropped her pack, motioning Arine to do the same. "Take the torch, Arine. I know where I'm going. It's not narrow for very long. I'll get in, then hand me the packs one at a time. Once they're through, you come through." Mestra moved towards the opening, sliding through the tight space.

Arine waited, her ears alert to any sound outside the crackle of the torch. Mestra's hand appeared, and Arine handed one of the packs to her. It disappeared into the rock. A few minutes later, the process was repeated. Taking a deep breath, Arine squeezed herself into the small crevice. She felt someone take the torch from her, freeing her hand to help propel her forward. Slowly, Arine emerged into a larger cavern.

Taking a moment to look around, Arine stared in amazement at the thousands of crystals that reflected the torchlight. The green and purple gems glittered all over the ceiling and walls. The floor itself was clear of them, except for a single large clear gem in the center of the room. It shone brighter than the rest. Mestra stood near it, the packs at her feet.

"What is this place?" Arine whispered, her voice tinged with awe.

"One of Sanctuary's best kept secrets. The miners who found this were among the first to come to Sanctuary. They thought to protect their claim against Domine Grace's taxes. They still come on occasion, taking a few gems at a time as is needed to do trade for themselves or Sanctuary." Arine watched as Mestra bent down and placed the torch in a set of iron rings rising from the ground. "We can rest here without any concern. It's best we keep traveling at night for a while yet."

Arine pulled herself away from the glittering walls and followed Mestra's lead, pulling out her bedroll and some food. "Where are we going, Mestra?"

"The port city of Dawnbreak, Domine Grace's main seat of power." Mestra paused, pushing at a stray lock of brown hair. "Ian's there. Mistress Bryn wasn't certain if he was within the palace itself or just in the city, however, so we'll have to do some looking."

Arine nibbled at some bread, trying to resist blurting out all her questions at once. "Why is he there? Did Mistress Bryn say where he's been or anything?"

"From what she could tell, the caravan Ian was sold to went to the Far Lands. Domine Grace is hosting a celebration in honor of the marriage of

Domine Elsa. She brought in people from the Far Lands to provide entertainment. Ian was among those who came." Arine started to ask a question, but Mestra held up a hand to stop her. "No, Arine, I don't know what kind of 'entertainment.' Nor does Mistress Bryn. She was able to learn there was a young man that had great talent as an artist with them. He met Ian's physical description, was mute, and would be the right age to be your brother."

Arine's heart skipped a beat. "Who did Elsa marry? Certainly not Cavon." She let a small chuckle escape her throat. "Or did she marry someone and insist the boy play part in her newest charade?"

Mestra laughed a bit, but there was little mirth in it. "She married James. Talia's been appointed to her council."

Snorting in disgust, Arine reached for her waterskin. "The Council should've let me kill her when I had the chance. They never should've given her time to run before meeting me in the Ring."

"I agree with you there, Arine. That's one of the reasons why Mistress Bryn sent both of us. Getting Ian out is a priority, yes, but we must silence Talia and James if at all possible. They know too much of how to get into and out of Sanctuary for us to let them go about in the world."

71

Arine lowered herself to the floor, trying to put the pieces together logically. With the knowledge, she was able to put her excitement in the background, focus on the mission ahead. It wasn't the time to give into her emotions. She regained her objectivity, which was going to be critical during the task ahead of them. "I've never been to Dawnbreak. Is it as big as they say? The sea, I mean."

"Bigger, most likely. You can't see the end of it from the docks. It stretches out, becomes one with the rising sun. When the first rays hit the water at dawn, it's like a million gems out on the water. I was never brave enough to set foot on one of the ships, let alone take a voyage. There's something about not seeing land that terrifies me to the very depths of my soul. Give me dirt and grass between my toes. The ones that live on the water are a different breed of women."

"Ian and I had never been. Mother never took us. And you say he's part of a group from the Far Lands?" Arine struggled with the idea of her brother, barely ten, facing a voyage like that.

"That's what Mistress Bryn found out. Between his talent to draw, being mute, and his coloring, I'd imagine he would've been a rare purchase at the market for visiting..." Mestra's voice trailed off, her focus shifting to the entrance to the small enclave.

The smell of smoke reached Arine's nose, but it didn't come from the torch in the room. The faint glow of light filled the narrow opening. Arine was on her feet, daggers at the ready. Motioning to Mestra, they each took up position on each side of the opening. Backs flattened against the crystals as best they could, they waited for the newcomers with weapons at the ready.

The torch emerged first. Arine glanced towards Mestra, nodding once. She'd do the first attack, stunning the person coming in. Then her friend would deal with whoever followed.

Shifting her stance slightly, she reached forward and grabbed the hand holding the torch by the wrist. With a single pull, she propelled the stranger into the room. He tripped on the uneven ground, falling with a grunt. Confident that Mestra would deal with the next intruder, she focused on the dark-haired man on the floor.

"I missed you too, Arine." Logan spoke quietly from his knees. With a sigh, he faced her.

Arine dropped her guard. "Logan? What are you doing here?!"

"What are either of you doing here?" Mestra's voice held little happiness.

73

Arine turned and saw Cavon pinned to the ground, her friend with a knee in his back.

"We talked with Mistress Bryn when you left. Convinced her we could help. And we can help." Logan looked up at her, his face insistent.

"Where we're going is dangerous for the two of you. Even if you don't use magic, you could be exposed. Domine Elsa will be there, along with Talia and James. There's going to be people who will recognize you. And us. You're going to be in our way more than helping us," Arine answered. "We don't have time to babysit the two of you. There's no way we could possibly get you into the city."

"That's not true, Arine. Now, hear me out," Mestra cut off her protest before she could voice it. "They're liabilities, yes. It'll make it harder for us to maneuver. But Bryn wouldn't have told them enough to find us if she didn't agree to this. There's a few precautions we can take, cover stories we can invent for the two of them during the road ahead." She turned her focus to the two men sitting on the floor. "Let me make one thing perfectly clear, though. I'm in charge. If I tell you to do something, you do it. You do not argue, you do not question. It is done. Got it?"

Chapter Nine

They smelled the sea long before they saw it. The air changed, taking on a salty aroma that was new to Arine. Mestra sniffed once, and muttered something about how some things never change.

For Arine, though, this was new. She kept in step with her friend, even as her eyes searched the horizon around every bend or crest of a small hill. She wanted to see the ocean. It had kept her and Ian apart for so long now. And, with luck, it would be the instrument used in reuniting them.

Mestra paused at a rock, making a show of pulling off her boot as other travelers passed them by. The road had gotten busy over the last day. Merchants and noblewomen flocked to the city for the festival Domine Grace had announced to celebrate her counterpart and ally's wedding.

"When we make it around this next bend, you'll see the city and the sea. This isn't a vacation; it's a job. Keep yourselves together, all of you. We've got a safe house to stay in until we head back. But we need to get there before dark. The streets here won't be safe for the boys at night." Mestra spoke low as she adjusted the laces on her boots.

"Daytime's still not good, but at night…best not to even try it."

"What happens at night?" Logan asked.

Mestra raised her head. "Ever been attacked, Logan? Followed because a woman thought you were pretty and wouldn't take no for an answer? Beaten or robbed because you're a boy and make for an easy mark? This isn't a farm. It's a city. The women down here are mean. They'll drug you, beat you, call you names just for entertainment. Because you're a boy. Do us all a favor. Keep close to us and keep your mouth shut." She stood up. "The only boys who are on the street after nightfall either belong to someone with power, or are being sold by the hour or act. You don't want to be mistaken for one of them."

Arine watched Logan's face, the reality of what was ahead of them sinking in. He was scared. Good. He needed to be. While he wasn't in a great situation when she fetched him years ago, it wasn't nearly as bad as what might happen.

Mestra rose from the rock, "Let's go. We're barely going to make it before sunset as it is."

As her friend promised, Arine's first sight of the sea was around the next bend. The rays of the sun glinted off an endless expanse of blue-green, sparkling more than the stars at night. Willing herself to keep moving forward, Arine swallowed the fear that came with seeing such an expanse. The Far Lands were on the other side, so it didn't go on forever. It just looked that way.

The road began a slow descent into the city below. Excitement threatened to overtake her outward calm. Arine focused on the road under her feet instead of the infinite horizon.

Dawnbreak sprawled along the shores of the sea. The buildings ranged from small homes and shops to domed towers and keeps, all laid out with straight streets heading in orderly directions. The layout was well planned. All roads led to the piers, where tall masted ships bobbed gracefully against wooden docks. Colorful banners hung from high windows and draped across rooftops. Arine cursed under her breath. The silk fabric looked beautiful, but it also discouraged someone like her from taking a different route to their destination. Even the nimblest thief, or Moreja, would find that way dangerous.

"I know, Arine. I wouldn't be surprised if the rooftop banners were Talia's idea. She knows how good you are at that sort of thing, and isn't as stupid as we'd like to hope. She's going to know we're coming for her eventually."

Arine nodded at Mestra's words. "She does. The moment she lost her bid and the council voted in our favor, she knew she was doomed. The Moreja don't treat traitors well." She glanced back at Logan and Cavon. "At least the beards hide their appearance a little. Not much. We're going to need them to stay inside as much as possible. It's one thing if we're spotted. If they are…". Her voice trailed off.

"It won't go well for them." Mestra finished the thought. "Think they'll listen if we tell them to stay inside? They're both rather stubborn."

Arine shrugged. "We can try. Logan does listen to me most of the time, and your warning scared him. Cavon, though. He's lived in a big city, yes. But he was sheltered, coddled. I don't think he was ever given permission to visit the darker parts."

"The safe house is centrally located, which benefits us. Right off one of the major open market areas." She pointed towards an open area in the city below. "It's not near enough to the docks for them to hear or see any of the auctions, but we still need to be careful. The local traders are just as likely to canvas the markets for unattached pretty boys as they are to be watching the ones they already own."

The terrain changed; packed dirt being replaced by cobblestones. As the road widened, the slope became steeper. A heavy rope, strung waist high alongside the road, assisted them as they wove their way down into the city itself.

Mestra led, and Arine positioned herself at the back so she could watch the boys and not lose sight of them. The press of people grew as they passed merchants set up on the side of the entry, attempting to pressure them into buying a few souvenirs of the momentous occasion before they entered the city gates. Arine kept a wary eye out as children darted between the masses, watching for pickpockets and cutpurses. Or Talia.

The guards merely noted the number of people entering the city. No one asked for names or city of origin. Domine Grace wanted everyone in her area to come celebrate. That alone alerted Arine that something else was happening. Grace had never been anything but cautious. She knew who lived in her lands, the comings and goings out of the city. Every ship, every horse, every cart was accounted for. Seaports were notorious for smuggling, and Domine Grace had a reputation of coming down hard on those who did so. At least, without bribing her first. As long as she got her due, she turned a blind eye to how the monies were gotten. Or who was leaving on the ships.

Arine kept pace, her eyes taking in alleyways and overhangs--any possible place for either an ambush or escape. They were now in enemy territory. Every mission encompassed the same risk, and she was well trained to know how to leave a place faster than she got into it.

Mestra stopped before a house, the smooth plaster painted a pretty yellow. A single wooden door, dark with iron hinges, sat between two large windows. Above, an iron railed balcony held nothing but a couple of flowering plants hanging off the side. Arine turned her attention away from the merchants closing up shop in the huge open area behind them as her friend pulled on a cord snaking from a hole in the wall near the door.

The door opened slightly, and Arine could barely make out the figure of a young boy, about ten.

"We are friends of Sabine's. She's expecting us." Mestra's voice was low.

The boy closed the door. "We wait. He went to get her."

"Friends of Sabine's, huh? Since when did she start taking in boys this old?" A snide voice came from the street.

Arine turned to face the speaker. Dark skinned, with her hair pulled back, the woman smiled at her. "If she's not willing to buy them, I will. I've got clients that like them a bit older." She thrust a chin towards Logan and Cavon.

"Sorry, but they're not up for sale. We have need of them yet." Arine kept her voice friendly.

"If you change your mind or finish with them, let me know. As long as they're not permanently damaged, that is. My name's Martine. I'm not hard to find."

"Martine, aren't you a bit far from the docks?" Another voice chimed in. Arine turned her head. Standing in the doorway was a blonde headed woman, her hands on her hips.

"Ships came in empty, Sabine. A woman's gotta find a way to fill them, right? Lots of people coming in for the party. Some might need money to get home with."

"Not these, Martine." Sabine stepped aside from the entry, waving a hand in welcome. "Come in, my sisters. We've been too many years apart."

Following the others inside, Arine looked over her shoulder as they entered.

Martine stood on the street, watching the door close behind them.

"Sorry about her, Mestra. Martine normally stays in the port district. The Far Lands must be desperate for boys, though. All the traders stay there, but she's been wandering around the market for a week or more now. Haven't seen her actually make a deal yet," Sabine said as she led them through a corridor towards the rear of the house.

The corridor opened up to a central garden. A balcony above them overlooked the lush plant life before them. On the other end of the garden stood a pair of spiraling stairs. "I've got a set of rooms set aside for you and your boys. Mistress Bryn gave me some details, and I've been able to learn more since she said you were coming. Once you've rested and bathed, we'll eat. Then we can talk."

"You have more information on Ian?" Arine couldn't help the hopeful tone from creeping into her voice.

Mestra glared at her, then replied to Sabine. "It's your house, my friend. We'll abide by your rules, even if we're anxious to get on with the mission. You take a great risk housing us, and we would not put you out more than we already have."

Arine bristled at the rebuke, but understood. She had crossed the line. Mestra was on lead for this, and with good reason.

Sabine smiled, "No apology necessary, my friend. And the risk is small. Domine Grace and I are on good terms. My account with her is more than current, and she knows it. She tends not to ask who stays at my home. Bryn let me know the circumstances, so Arine's question is not out of line." She continued to speak as she led them up one of the staircases. "However, your journey here has been long. The caves, while excellent for travelling safely, are not equipped for bathing. The boys with you may need to rest while we speak, as well. I can't imagine the journey was easy for them. Ah, here we are." She stopped in front of a door painted a bright red, with brass fittings. "Here's the key," placing an item in Mestra's hand, "and the bath is off the main room. There's a couple of sleeping alcoves as well. I'll send up Brian in a few hours when dinner is ready."

Outwardly, Arine kept her composure as their host left them and she followed Mestra into the room. Inwardly, however, her thoughts and emotions churned like never before. So close to seeing Ian again, convincing him to join her in a life better than whatever he must've led for the last decade.

The room was well furnished, a creative mix of functional chairs and tables and large cushions. The tranquil blues and greens didn't help her regain her composure. She knew she had to be calm, for all their sakes. It wasn't just her she'd be putting in danger this trip if she couldn't remember her training.

She began a customary sweep of the room, checking for everything from hidden doors to secret observation holes. Mestra's voice, while low, carried well in the room. The acoustics were such that any small noise would be heard by them. All the worse for anyone who would try to sneak in while they slept.

"Get a grip on yourself, Arine. You're worse than a new Sister on their first mission." Mestra's voice held a slight rebuke. "You know any information Sabine has will wait until she's ready to tell us. Bryn trusts her. So do I. That should be enough."

Arine picked up the muted sounds of water. The boys were bathing. Good. They tended to get grouchy after a few days without. While she was content with waiting another month if it meant Ian was safe at last.

She sank into one of the central chairs, tossing one of the overstuffed pillows onto the floor. "I know, Mestra. I didn't think it would be this hard, not after this long. What if he doesn't recognize me? Or it's not him?"

"Then we still offer him Sanctuary and get our asses home. And Bryn will keep searching." Mestra shrugged. "I know you're hopeful, Arine. We all are or we wouldn't have come with you. But you have to put it aside for now. You celebrate when we're back home, and not before."

Arine rubbed her forehead with her fingers. A dull headache threatened to increase in intensity. "I know. To celebrate early means death. For me, for the one I was sent to fetch, for those risking the journey with me. But..." her voice trailed off.

"No 'buts,' Arine. Once the boys are done, we'll clean up. Go eat dinner with Sabine. Learn what she has to tell us. Then we rest until tomorrow."

"And tomorrow?"

Mestra smiled slightly, "Tomorrow, we let you see your brother. And figure out what damage Talia's done."

* * *

A youth, barely old enough to shave, carefully placed a steaming bowl of soup in front of Arine. The aromas drifting up from the dish made her mouth water. "I had the same meal we're going to eat prepared and taken up to your boys, Mestra. I'm sure they're hungry, after the long journey here," Sabine said, her spoon poised above her own bowl.

"I'm sure they'll appreciate it, once they wake up." Mestra chuckled a little. "It took them less than five minutes after they got out of the bath to find a bed and fall asleep."

Arine kept her eyes on her food, savoring the warm broth. She hated to admit it, but the idea of sleeping on a bed and not the hard earth appealed to her right now.

Sabine and Mestra kept a steady stream of conversation going throughout the first course, mainly focusing on various events Domine Grace had scheduled around the city for the celebration. Arine tuned most of it out, trusting her friend would let her know of anything of concern when they were alone again. Instead, she focused on the room itself. The windows seemed oddly placed. While she could see people on the street below moving about, the image seemed oddly distorted.

"It's because you're seeing a reflection, Arine." Sabine's voice cut through her thoughts.

Blinking, she turned her attention to their host. "A reflection? How?"

Sabine sat back slightly, allowing the servant to clear her bowl for the next course. "I have a series of mirrors set up, allowing us to see who and what goes on down on the street, but they can't see who my guests are. It was costly, but has repaid me several times over. I frequently host people who, like yourselves, don't necessarily want their visit to Dawnbreak to be of public record."

A new plate, one of roasted beef, potatoes, and vegetables drenched in a cream sauce, was placed in front of her. "Would you object if I examined it closer? A system like this could help strengthen Sanctuary." Arine asked, as she began to eat.

Sabine smiled, "Not at all. I'll do you one better. I'll get a second set of blueprints made tonight for you to take back with you. They should be ready before the sitting tomorrow."

Arine started a little, "What sitting?"

Sabine looked up at the servant in the room, "You're dismissed. We'll take care of things from here." Then waited as the room cleared and it was just the three of them.

"The boy we believe to be your brother is here from the Far Lands. He came with a group of artists, and there's been an announcement made that he is available for private portraits. I've made an appointment for tomorrow, here in my home. Once he's set up his equipment, I'll make sure any accompanying people are removed from the room and you'll go in. The sitting's only supposed to last for an hour, and he has to have some work done or it'll look suspicious. You'll have that time to confirm he is your brother, and convince him to come back with you. The following day, when he comes back for the follow-up sitting, is when we'll smuggle you all back out of town."

Mestra coughed, "I like the plan, Sabine. Except it doesn't give us much time to figure up what Talia's up to."

"What's there to figure out with her? She's here with Domine Elsa and convinced her to marry James instead of Cavon. You really don't think she's not told her all she knows about Sanctuary, do you?"

Mestra sighed, "No, not really. Not if she wants to live. She may have held back a little information, something critical, that would keep her safe from Domine Elsa's vengeance. I imagine the Domine wasn't thrilled when Talia's original try at taking over Sanctuary failed."

Sabine nodded, "Exactly. Maybe she doesn't know about the tunnels, or the small caves where you sleep. But everything else she does. Don't delude yourself. The first day those two appeared in the city, Talia looked beaten. And James had all the earmarks of a terrified boy. Elsa doesn't take disappointment well." She pushed her chair back, rising gracefully. "Tomorrow, Mestra, you and the boys can accompany me to the market right here while Arine's talking with our other guest. Keep your eyes open; see if you can learn anything else. I don't trust Domine Grace's apparent lack of security. She's working on something. I just don't know what yet. But I wouldn't unpack your bags if I were you."

Arine rose as their host left the room. Mestra nodded once, and she followed her friend back to their room. If anything more was going to be discussed, it would be there.

* * *

Hours later, as the twin moons came close to meeting, she knelt before the altar set off from the main gardens. She'd never been one for prayer, really. Tonight, when she was this close to fulfilling the promise she made to herself and Cinphire a decade ago, it seemed appropriate.

A light breeze wafted through the small chapel, tickling her nose with the sweet jasmine and lilac blooms from the garden nearby.

Arine knelt in silence, her heart speaking more than she could voice. *I know not why he was taken, or why it took ten years to find him, but on this night, I thank you for allowing me to bring him home at last.*

The breeze shifted. A hint of honey mixed with a familiar muskiness brought a smile to her face. Without opening her eyes, she spoke, "What woke you, Logan?"

"You weren't there. It worried me." She heard him slide onto a bench behind her. "To be honest, I'm surprised you were here. It's not a place where I would expect to find you." He kept his voice low.

She opened her eyes, gazing at the porcelain figure before her. "With the meeting tomorrow, being so close to finally bringing Ian home, it seemed to be the place to be." She touched her finger to her lip, then placed it on the breast of the statue in silent benediction. Only then did she rise and look at Logan.

She saw him for the first time, really. Not his physical form, but the patience. The love and devotion he had for her, for her quest. The realization that he'd spent the last years of his life taking care of her. So she could do her job. So she could bring Ian home.

It was time. "Logan," she said, as she knelt in front of him and took his huge hands into her own, "you've been far more patient than I deserve. I wouldn't be here if not for you. If you're willing, when we get home again, will you stand in front of Mistress Bryn with me and seal yourself to me?"

She knew his answer before he voiced it. The glow of happiness that exploded on his face told her she'd almost waited too long. "I…yes. At the date and time of your choosing. I will be there." His face split into a grin.

She reached up and gave him a gentle kiss. "Now, let's go back to bed. The news can wait until later."

Chapter Ten

Arine took a deep breath, trying to calm her nerves. Was it nerves? She wasn't sure. Excitement might have been a better word. She could hear the muted voices on the other side of the door. Any moment now, Sabine would let her in. To meet Ian. To talk him into coming home to Sanctuary with her.

Mestra spoke low, "I'll be right out here when you're done. Just knock on the door. Sabine's taking the boys into the market and gave the staff time off. It'll be just the two of you in there. His escort is waiting outside the other side of the room, though, so keep your voice down."

She nodded once, not trusting her own voice. *Damn it, Arine,* she swore to herself. *It's like all the others you've done. Get your focus in place and treat him like the rest.*

Only she knew she was lying to herself. It wasn't like all the others. This was Ian. The one job she wanted more than any others.

The door opened slightly and Sabine slid through the crack, closing it behind her. "He's ready, Arine. Make the most of your time. His escort wasn't pleased to be told to wait outside during the session. When the hour is up, she'll be knocking to come in. You have to finish convincing him by then, set up a cover for him to come back tomorrow. Or it won't work."

Arine watched her walk past her towards where Logan stood with Cavon. He smiled at her, and she took one more deep breath before opening the door before her.

Sunlight filtered through the light-colored curtains, bathing the room in a pale green glow. Across the room, an easel was set up. The canvas blocked the figure behind it, but she could hear him. His hands peeked around the left as he set a small roll of cloth on a table next to him. She moved across the carpeted floor. He was expecting someone. But would he realize who she was?

Finally, she couldn't wait any longer. She had to see his face. Working her way around the edge of his artist's space, she waited for him to turn around.

He was taller. That was the first thing she noticed. She chided herself at the surprise. It'd been ten years. Of course he was taller. His hair, always a shade or two lighter than hers, shone a bright red in the filtered light.

She didn't make a sound, but waited. A second or two passed before he stopped unpacking the small kit of supplies and straightened. He knew she was there.

He turned to face her, his eyes going to the floor. At the same time, her heart soared. There was no doubt now.

"Hello, Ian," she whispered.

He brought his gaze up to meet hers at the sound of her voice. It took him a moment, but she saw the disbelief play across his face as he recognized her at last.

"Arine?" his soft voice trembled as he said her name.

She laughed, holding out her arms to welcome his embrace. Holding him tight, she marveled again at how tall he'd gotten. She let herself have a moment to revel in knowing he was real and with her again.

"Ian, I need to talk to you." She broke from the hug and led him towards a divan. "I know, we've got so much time to catch up on. I want to know everything you've been through from the moment Ma sold you. But it has to wait."

She watched his face intently, scanning it for any signs of confusion. "I left after I came home and found out what she did to you. I was determined to find you, keep you safe. Whatever horrors you've endured since that moment are my fault for not finding you sooner." She took his hands into his. "I ended up at Sanctuary, Ian. And

94

they helped me find you. That's why I'm here. I want to take you home. You'll be free…" Arine broke off as he took his hands from hers and rose.

"Arine, you don't understand." He went back to his supplies and picked up a piece of charcoal. Sketching as he spoke, he explained, "I have to do a sketch or people will wonder. But we can talk while I do this."

She sat; her forehead creased in confusion. "What don't I understand, Ian? I'm offering you a chance to be safe, get out from under the thumb of whoever's using your talent for their gain."

His hand flew across the canvas. "But no one is, Arine. Things are different over in the Far Lands. Men have a voice in what happens to them. I get to keep my money. Around here, we keep up appearances. But back there, even once we're on the ship home, it's different." He paused, focusing on the stroke of his hand.

"What are you saying? You want to stay?"

He looked at her, his face a conflict of emotions. "I have a good life now. When I first went there, I was scared. I didn't want to talk to anyone. I just drew my pictures and hoped someone would pay me with food. That's when I met Caroline."

Arine kept her focus on her brother, watching the changes on his face. There wasn't any of the fear she normally saw on the boys she'd fetched. Or hope for the new life she promised. There was excitement for seeing her, yes. But there was also happiness.

"Well, it was her mother I met at first. She saw me trying to sell some portraits in a market, hired me to do one of her daughters. She fed me, gave me a room, everything. By the time Caroline returned a few days later, I wasn't a street urchin any more. They let me stay there, helped me build a reputation with my art. Coaxed me out of my shell."

His hand flew across the canvas as fast as Arine's heart sank. "About five years ago, she asked me to join with her, be her mate. We've got twins, a girl and a boy, that are two now. We left them back home."

"If it's so good there, why come here?" She had to ask. "Why risk being sold again?"

Ian's face softened. "Caroline is good friends with a captain, someone who buys boys from here and frees them when they get across the ocean. She's been helping us try and find you."

A chuckle escaped her throat. "Find me? Why?"

"I know what Ma was like, Arine. If you'd stayed, it wouldn't have been for long. You had no interest in taking on the business, tanning leather. And she never cared about anything but what she wanted. With how good things are, all I could think of was bringing you to my new home."

Arine lowered her head, her mind trying to contemplate what he was saying. That's when it hit her. As much as he wouldn't leave his life, his love, she couldn't leave hers.

"I can't, Ian. Any more than you can. I love what I do, bringing boys to Sanctuary. Saving them. I'm good at it. There's so many out there who didn't get lucky like you. And then there's Logan."

Ian's face brightened, "I'm glad, Arine. More than you can imagine. All I've hoped for over the years is to learn you're happy." He shifted his stance. "Caroline's here, outside. Would you like to meet her?"

Arine smiled as her heart sat like lead in her chest.

Chapter Eleven

Logan watched Arine walk into the room. This meant so much to her. If only he could be there with her. But she had to meet Ian alone. There'd be time for him to get to know her brother on the way home.

"Come on, Logan. They're leaving us behind." Cavon's voice pulled his attention away from the closed door. "Stop thinking about your fiancée and let's go."

He felt his face heat up. They'd shared the news with Mestra and Cavon that morning. But it was still new, strange to hear. "Yeah, I know." He turned and followed his friend towards an open door.

Bright sunlight bathed the courtyard. Sabine waited for them, but not patiently. "Keep up. Arine's only got an hour in there and I've got to get things ready for after you leave. There's an expectation of hosting during a celebration of this magnitude that I can't hide from." She walked briskly over to a tall gate to the right of the house. Unlocking it, she spoke quietly, "Stay close while we're in the market. You can look around, but I can't guarantee your safety if you wander too far. This is one of the better ones, but it can be rough some days."

Logan glanced over at Cavon, puzzled. "Rough?"

Sabine turned to face them as she pulled the gate open. "Let's just say that the women around here appreciate boys and aren't shy about expressing it." She walked through the portal, not bothering to look back to make sure they followed.

Unlike when they'd arrived the day before, the market was in full swing. Dozens of stalls crowded next to each other, doing their best to tempt customers to come buy their wares. Vibrant bolts of cloth were displayed alongside exotic fruits that Logan couldn't put a name to.

"Hey, it's a chandler. You should go talk shop." Cavon pointed to a stall not far down the row. Freshly poured candles hung from lines of hemp. The woman in the stall, clearly the shop owner, was watching a small boy intently as he carefully placed tapers for sale.

"Something tells me she wouldn't want to talk to me unless I was buying." Logan turned, taking in the market as a whole.

"If I had something that nice, I'd never let you out in public." A female voice called out, followed by a long whistle.

Logan whipped his head around, trying to pinpoint the speaker. She leaned against a wall, leering at him.

"I can give you whatever your momma won't, sweetie." She winked at him.

Someone tugged at his arm. Cavon whispered, "Ignore them, Logan. They're only trying to get you to react." He pulled him forward.

"Aww, baby. Don't be leaving so soon! Smile and decorate the world a bit longer." The woman called out again.

Another woman stopped in front of them. "Running away already? What's wrong, little boys? Too good for the likes of us?" She stood with her hands on her hips. Thrusting her chin forward, she sneered, "Ain't no one around here that's gonna do anything you don't want. We just gotta warm you up to the idea."

A black arm, decorated with gold bangles, dropped between Logan and the woman in front of him. Martine's voice, still full of disdain, was low. "Back off, Dawn. These two are mine already. I'm talking with Sabine. So, unless you want to come to terms with me…"

Dawn backed away; her hands raised. "Didn't mean no harm, Martine. Woman sees something fine come down the road, she has to express her appreciation." The woman made an obvious show of looking the boys over from head to toe. Logan repressed a shiver as she leered at him.

"Martine, I told you. They're with me. Not for sale." Sabine appeared out of nowhere, shoving packages at Logan and Cavon.

Hurriedly, Logan reached out to grab the items before they fell to the ground. His hands shook, his stomach churned. Fear threatened to take hold.

"I know that, Sabine. I'm thinking of leaving earlier than planned. Maybe even sailing tonight. Are you sure I can't get you to give me a good price on these two? The Far Lands are always looking for healthy boys."

"No, Martine. They're not mine to sell. Maybe you should look at the market by the East Gate. I hear they're letting just about anyone in for the celebration."

Martine turned and shrugged. "Too crowded. West gate seems to be good, though. The big unveiling of the groom is tomorrow night. Should be even more arriving today than yesterday." She strode off without another word.

Logan managed to get the last parcel secured in his hands just as Sabine looked at him. "We need to go back. Now."

Without a word, the two followed their hostess back to the safety of her home.

Sabine set a brisk pace, surprising Logan. He and Cavon darted around people in the path, juggling packages while keeping pace. With each step, his alarm grew. What had happened? By the time they reached the gated courtyard, his mind was awash with theories. Was it Arine? Was the artist not Ian?

A young boy waited at the door into the home, his arms outstretched for the packages he and Cavon carried. Logan hurried, cursing at how tangled his fingers had gotten in the cords. He darted inside just as Sabine went into the room where Arine last was. Mestra followed on her heels, closing the door behind them.

His mind raced. Something happened, and it probably had to do with Arine. He no longer cared about what was and wasn't allowed in this city. He reached out for the knob.

"Logan, what are you doing? We can't just walk in there." Cavon's voice hissed the warning. "Who knows what's wrong. But this is Sabine's house, it's not Sanctuary. Here were can't just…"

Logan turned, leveling a steely gaze at his friend. "I know. But I also need to know what happened. You saw Sabine's face, how fast she pushed to get back here. I need to make sure Arine's not hurt. I--"

The knob twisted beneath his hand. Startled, he let go and stepped back as the door swung open. Mestra looked at him, her face a mask. "You can come in. She wants you to meet him."

Logan nodded and moved past Mestra into the room. His eyes scanned the room, searching for Arine.

She sat on the edge of a sofa. Across from her were two strangers. He had no idea who the woman was. The boy, though--there was no mistaking the family resemblance.

"Logan, come here and meet Ian." Arine's voice was low. Excitement played across her face, with something else he couldn't quite pinpoint. Still, he moved closer as she reached out her hand.

"Ian, this is Logan. Logan, this is Ian. And his wife, Caroline."

That's when he caught it. The slight tone of disappointment, of loss. The meeting had not gone as she'd hoped. As they all hoped.

Sabine stepped forward, "I hate to interrupt, but things are in motion. They need to leave now, Arine, if they're to make it."

Logan looked from Sabine to Arine, puzzled. "Leave now? Why?"

Arine smiled at him. "They're heading back to their ship for the night, Logan. And we've been promised the chance to see the best beach you can imagine. But we have to leave now, if we're to get back before the gates close for the night."

He nodded, the knot in his stomach tightening. Her words didn't ring true, but he knew she'd not say anything different if he asked. If, when he needed to know, she'd tell him. And not a moment before. That secrecy was part of her job, of her.

"Well, then, do I need to go change?" he asked, hoping that Sabine thought he believed the lie. For all their sakes, he had to convince anyone that asked.

Chapter Twelve

Arine embraced Ian one more time. "I'm glad we met again, Ian. Even if it's to say goodbye." Without a look back, she turned and walked from the room. As she did, she let go of the last decade and all the uncertainty. He may not be coming home with her, but she knew he had a good life where he was. In that way, it wasn't a wasted trip.

Inside, frustration warred with reason. He had a good life, and she was glad for that. But she knew it would take time before she stopped wondering if she could've said something else to change his mind. Ten years of hoping, searching, was not something she could let go of easily.

Then there was the look on Sabine's face when she entered the room. The whispered conversation to Mestra. Something had happened. And they had to move. Now. The information Sabine had given her was no information at all. Nothing more than a hasty, "You leave now. No questions." And she had to abide by that. Mestra's slight nod was enough to tell her the situation was dire.

Without glancing back, she strode from the room. Further instruction was needed, but Arine chafed at the idea that she wasn't in charge once again. No wonder Mistress Bryn sent her out alone so often. Second fiddle was not a position that sat well with her.

She waited with the others for Sabine and Mestra to join them. Logan's face was flushed. Had something happened in the market? *Goddess, I hope he didn't use his magic*, she thought. The whole mission was lost if he did. Even if Talia didn't know they were there yet, that would surely get back to her. And faster than a flame on a field of dry grass.

Mestra approached them. "We're heading to the gate. Sabine's getting horses ready for us now. No time to grab gear. It's already been sent ahead and will be waiting for us." She paused. "If the guards ask, we're taking the boys to the beach. Sabine's going to do most of the talking, so just act like you want to get there. Don't overthink it."

Arine nodded in understanding. Explanations now would take too long. She'd been in a hurry to leave somewhere too often not to recognize the signs.

Without further delay, they made their way to the courtyard. Sabine already on her horse. Three more mounts, saddled and with grooms beside them to assist, waited for them. Sabine's face welcomed no questions. Silently, Arine prayed that Logan had an idea of how to ride. He grew up on a farm, yes, but that was a lifetime ago.

Sabine kept a slow but steady pace, threading their way through the crowded streets. Arine kept alert, but relaxed. Her eyes darted about, never staying on one thing or person for long. Running now would not guarantee anything but attention being brought to them.

Mestra rode next to her. Her voice, quiet, barely reached Arine's ear. "There was an incident in the market. Nothing more than Cavon could handle, but Logan was uncomfortable. Martine was there. Sabine wasn't thrilled with what she said, knew it was time to get us out. Before it was too late."

Arine replied, her eyes focused on Logan's back as he rode in front of her. "Too late for what?"

"Too late to get out. The gates are being sealed at dusk. If we don't leave now, we're going to have Talia and the Domine's personal guard at our throats by midnight."

Arine nodded once. If Sabine said it was time to go, it was. Her thoughts moved to Ian and his wife. She made a silent prayer to the Goddess to guide them safely back to their ship. And that the captain was a good woman who wouldn't hand them over at the first sign of trouble.

It took them longer than she liked to weave through the throngs of people. Time wasn't on their side to begin with, not if the guards would believe the outing ruse.

By the time the gate came into view, Arine's muscles ached from the tension. Outwardly, she knew she appeared relaxed. Calm. Everything was normal. Only her companions knew she was ready to defend or run at the first sign of trouble.

A guard, her hair damp from the afternoon heat, raised a hand to halt Sabine's progress. Arine stopped as well, close enough to hear.

"My Lady, it's late for an excursion."

Sabine sighed, "I know, Elewys. It's the boys. They heard about a beach and have no idea what that is. They've been nagging us all morning to see one. You know how whiny they can get. I finally gave in just to get some peace. We're heading over to Melisandra's Point. It's not far. We'll be back before the celebration tonight."

Arine kept her eyes on the guard, waiting. Logan's voice carried past her ears, "Why aren't we at the beach yet?" His petulant tone had her lowering her head to hide the grin threatening to appear.

The guard grinned. "Just be sure to watch the time and don't let the boys talk you into staying too long. Domine Grace wouldn't be happy if you weren't there tonight." She stepped aside, waving off the other guards, and allowed them to pass through the gate.

Sabine kept a stately pace until they rounded a bend and left the sight of the gate. At that point, they spurred their mounts into a gallop. And headed towards the hill and hidden tunnel.

A small knot of people waited near the opening. Arine changed the reins over to her left hand before reaching into her boot with her right. The hilt of one of her throwing knives slid into her palm. Just in case.

A dark figure moved out from the center of the gathering. "About time you got here," Martine smiled at them as she reached for Sabine's horse. "I was starting to get worried."

Sabine didn't share her grin. "We moved as fast as we dared. Even then, we were questioned at the gate." She turned in her saddle. "Everyone dismount. Martine's associates will take care of the horses."

Arine started, her hand still on her blade. "Martine?"

The woman smiled at her. "Good to know my ruse worked so well. If you didn't suspect, I'm almost certain we've fooled Talia. I work for Mistress Amelia. She runs the Moreja in the Far Lands. I have to speak with Mistress Bryn, on matters we could not trust to be written down." She turned to Cavon and Logan, both of whom had eased off their horses. "My apologies if I offended you earlier. Sabine and I long ago figured out a way for me to pass information to her without it being intercepted. My words were for her, not because I thought poorly of you." She bowed in respect.

Arine dismounted, handing over the reins to one of Martine's guard. "If it's all a ruse…"

"Your brother is fine, Arine. He and his family came across on my ship, under my protection. They were back on board and raised anchor before you reached the gate. If things get unpleasant tonight, as we fear they will, they will be well out to sea and out of harm's way."

Sabine's horse danced nervously, and she brought him back under control. "I need to return now. I dare not be gone much longer. The gates are being sealed tonight, and the army will march through the city. Few won't be conscripted by morning."

Mestra looked at her. Arine took note of the hard line her jaw was set into. "The rumors were true, then?"

"Yes. Elsa talked Grace into joining her forces. Talia's told them everything. They'll move on Sanctuary before the end of the week. Move fast, through the tunnels. Get word to Bryn- -"

Her voice broke off. Arine watched in horror as a dark red stain began to seep across her bright yellow tunic. She slid sideways off her saddle, exposing the crossbow bolt sticking out of her back as she fell lifelessly to the ground.

"Inside! Now!" Mestra ordered. Arine took up a defensive posture as she scanned the horizon. Talia stood, surrounded by armed guards, fifty feet away.

"Best run, Arine! Or I'll put you each down one by one!" Talia's voice dripped hatred.

Arine stepped forward, her eyes fixed on her target. "You're the one that needs to run, Talia. Just like you did back in Sanctuary!"

Another crossbow bolt whistled past her shoulder as she made her advance. Arine didn't bother to see where it landed. Talia was close, and that was all that mattered. She was going to end this, once and for all.

"Arine!" Martine called out to her, but she continued her march forward.

"She's mine!" Talia growled, knocking away the crossbow being aimed her direction.

"Arine! We need you...please!" Logan's voice penetrated the rage that overtook her body.

She glanced back, and saw the bolt that now protruded from Mestra's shoulder. Cavon and Logan were holding her up, while Martine waved at her to join them. With a final glare of hatred towards Talia, she sprinted towards the cave.

Crossbow bolts shattered against the walls as they dove for cover. Arine led the way, knowing the best place to make their stand. The passageway narrowed and made a sharp bend, just enough for single combat. That would give them the advantage over Talia and her troops.

As they rounded the bend, she called out, "Cavon, there's a small crystal chamber fifteen feet further up. On the left. Take Mestra. Do what you must to heal her. Martine, you and I fight in rotation. Logan", she paused, "take Mestra's sword. If they get past us, you'll at least be able to defend yourself for a few moments."

She turned back towards the bend, her heart cold. There were only two of them, really. And she had no idea how skilled Martine was. She was a Moreja, yes. But so was Talia at one point.

She looked over at the dark-skinned woman. Her hands held the curved blade, the point low. Her face wore the same grim reality that Arine knew. This could be their final fight.

A hand touched her shoulder. Glancing back, she saw Logan standing there. "It won't come to that, Arine. I won't let it." He squeezed past her, moving towards the switchback.

She reached out to stop him, but he shrugged off her hand. "Stay back. I don't want you getting hurt." He smiled, then turned his head back to the wall of the tunnel. He reached his arms out to each side, a massive palm splayed out on the rock face.

"What's he doing?" Martine whispered.

Arine shook her head, "I don't know."

A low rumble reached her ears, followed by the ground shaking violently beneath her feet. Both grew in intensity, causing her to brace herself against the closest wall. The tunnel in front of Logan began to collapse. Massive rocks fell from the ceiling, kicking up dust and cutting off the feeble light filtering in from outside. She threw her arm across her face in an attempt to keep from breathing in the dust as the tunnel shuddered one final, massive time. The darkness became absolute.

She could hear Martine coughing when it was over. A spark in the dark near where Logan had been, followed by the rushing sound of flames eating at the ends of a torch. The light blended with the still settling dust, but she could see his face. He was tired, and there was fear in his eyes. She knew that look. Cavon had it after he'd healed her.

"By the Goddess, what did you do?" Martine's voice, barely above a whisper, carried both awe and anger.

Arine knew what he'd done. Whatever Sabine had told Martine about the boys, it probably wasn't the magic. "He did what he had to do to save us, Martine. As is Cavon. It's nothing to fear."

She reached out a hand, pulling Logan to her. Even with her own stomach threatening to revolt, she wouldn't let him see her fear. This was part of him, and she had to accept it.

"Let's go find Cavon and Mestra. We'll talk then. No one's going to come this way again for a long time."

Chapter Thirteen

Arine sat watch out of habit. Cavon and Mestra slept, both worn out from his healing. Martine had taken the news that the boys could work magic well. She was Moreja, though. They were trained to accept things they couldn't fully understand. It wasn't about hating differences, but embracing them.

She shifted her stance against the rock, willing her back to relax. With Logan sealing off the passage the way he did, it was highly unlikely they'd be disturbed. Talia and the Domines would have to march overland to reach Sanctuary, and that would take time. The tunnel provided the five of them with a faster route, giving Sanctuary time to prepare for whatever forces would come against them.

Someone moved, but she didn't look towards them. Her focus stayed on what might come at them.

"Have you eaten?" Logan asked. "I know you haven't slept."

Arine turned, smiling at him as he handed her a piece of bread and some cheese. Her stomach growled. "Thank you. Didn't know I was hungry until just now. Is that part of your magic?" She kept her voice light, teasing.

He chuckled. "No, not unless five years at your side counts. I know you, Arine. You're less likely to take care of yourself if there are others who need it more."

They stood, each against the small opening to the cave, eating. Something had been in Arine's mind for a while now, but she'd never asked. It seemed right to do so now.

"What's it like, Logan? Doing magic?"

He raised his head, but wouldn't look at her. "I'm not sure how to describe it, really. It's not like I get all tingly or anything. It's just, when I know someone I care about is going to be hurt, I have to do something. If I don't, I'll explode."

He faced her now, shadows from the torchlight highlighted his chiseled features. "I don't mean 'care' like love, Arine. You're the only one I love. But that's been the one common thread Cavon and I discovered while we talked with the older men in Sanctuary. The ones who remembered the wars from when they were very small. When magic was commonplace, before it was outlawed. The men who could do magic, it wasn't a lot of them. And they all cared very deeply about people. All people, not just nobles or their own families. When that began to be misused, abused, that's when things went wrong. There's a theory in one of the old books that women never developed magic because they only cared for their families. That they were just as afraid of their neighbors as they were someone like Martine from the Far Lands. Fear prevents us from doing so much. It's those who care without fear that can work miracles."

Arine listened to his words carefully. It made sense. "Do they think women could do magic, then? If they could ignore differences?"

He nodded. "Yes. The magic doesn't care if it's a man or woman wielding it. It was abused before, and won't be now. Neither Cavon or I can do it without need. Someone we care for must be in danger. From death, from being crushed or burned, something dire. I can't decide to do dishes without getting my hands wet." He chuckled.

"You talk like it's alive."

"It is. For me, at least. I won't say it's a voice in my head or anything like that. I'm not crazy. But it's very much alive. It went dormant after the wars. Too many men used it to destroy instead of protect. We're supposed to live together, not fear each

117

other. I don't think it'll let itself be used like that again."

"Have you ever tried? Doing the dishes without getting your hands wet?" She smiled. The two of them often worked as a team around the house, but he would tease her about his poor hands when she'd been gone.

He laughed again. "Once. It gave me a headache. That's when we started discussing the idea of it being alive. It's different for each of us. Cavon can heal wounds. I move things. There was one man we met, very ancient --he used to be able to create fire. One of the kings of old told him to use it to erect a wall of flame. Said it was to save them from death. Only it wasn't. There was a family inside the barn he surrounded with fire. The father had denied him a heirloom sword, so the king burned them all alive and took the weapon. As soon as the old man saw what he had been used for, he fled. Never called upon the magic again. And still won't. Says he's still paying penance for taking life instead of saving it."

"So, it won't let you kill now?" Silently, she hoped she knew the answer. It would solve so many problems if the Domines couldn't force Logan or Cavon to kill.

Logan shrugged, "I'm not sure. I mean, it was possible that some of Talia's troops had made it into the tunnel before I collapsed it, or that they were hit by rocks as they flew out the entrance. I wasn't trying to hurt anyone. Just wanted to keep you and the rest safe. I think it looks into my heart, sees my intent. If I wanted to do harm, it wouldn't have done what I did." He paused. "We pay a price for what we do, Arine. It's a physical one. The more we do, the harder it is to recover from. Cavon's going to be up and moving faster from repairing Mestra's shoulder than he was when he healed you. He talked about that, in the group. The poison had traveled extensively through your blood by the time he was able to get you to safety. It was embedding itself into the muscles, causing them to become paralyzed. It took more than he'd ever done before, and it weakened him for days. The pot I moved to save Julia left me a little dizzy. Today—well, you saw what I was like afterwards."

She remembered his ashen skin, the lines of sweat leaving traces through the dust on his face. How he leaned heavily on the wall on the way to this cavern, collapsing in a heap when they reached it. Only the rhythmic rise of his chest kept her from fearing the worst.

Reaching across the small space between them, she took his hand. "The collapse was that extensive, then? None will come from that direction tonight?"

"Yes. It will take months for the rubble to be cleared. Even then, it may rain even more of the mountain on their heads. I...I only wanted to keep you safe. You scared me, Arine. When you went after Talia. She had so many with her. The moment the fight went against her, she would've had them shower you with bolts. You weren't going to win because she wasn't going to fight fair." Tears welled up in his eyes. "I don't want to lose you, not like that. Not have you cut down while I watched."

She pulled him closer and placed one hand on his chest. "I didn't mean to make you afraid, Logan. If there's no way we'll be caught unawares, there's another cavern like this not far. Big enough for two." Arine placed a gentle kiss at the base of his throat. "Maybe there's a way I can make it up to you."

Chapter Fourteen

One thing about the tunnel and cave system had always bothered Arine. She couldn't keep track of time. Without the sun or stars, she couldn't keep her days and nights straight. Time was on their side right now. Talia would need to go overland, taking weeks to get to Sanctuary. The wagons, laden down with food and supplies for the army, would slow them down even further. But that didn't mean she felt no urgency. There were hundreds who needed as much warning as they could get. Sick, elderly, or young. The evacuation would take time to execute.

She had slept well, the warmth of Logan's body keeping the natural chill at bay. But now, she wanted to move.

Mestra awoke, her movements slow. Arine understood the feeling. Though she'd been passed out when Cavon worked on her. She couldn't fathom what it might have been like for her friend, being awake while enduring that.

"It didn't hurt, Arine. Not the healing anyway. Pulling out the bolt, well…"

Arine nodded in understanding. They both bore a few scars from that sort of encounter. The Moreja were trained to endure more pain than a lucky shot. But it still hurt.

"Are you up to travel today? When the others are awake?"

Mestra shifted her position on the floor, "Yes. We can't sit here for long. Not if our warning will have any real effect."

"Good. I think we need to push things, go as far as we can before we rest." She thrust her chin towards a small pile on the floor. "Martine was able to grab a pack or two on her way down the tunnel, but the rest were buried in the cave-in. We need to do inventory, see what we've got on hand. Last thing we need is to run out of water on the first day."

Mestra joined her by the pile and they began to rummage through the pockets, separating the various supplies. "Did you know? What Logan was going to do?" Mestra whispered.

Arine shook her head once, placing a spare tunic off to one side. "No. He didn't share his plan with us. Just told us to stay back. We talked some last night about it. What about Cavon?"

"He apologized a lot. Kept saying he was sorry for having to do the healing at all. I think it scares him."

"It scares both of them, though I think Logan's got a better handle on it. He's thought a lot on where the magic comes from, how it works. I'm not sure I understand it all. But it works for them. I'm grateful for what they did yesterday. I'd rather get home without needing more of it, though."

"Agreed." They sorted in silence for a few moments. "How are things with you and Logan now? I saw your face briefly when you joined us here. There was fear on it."

Arine sighed. "I admit, it was strange to see him do that. Mistress Bryn told me, yes. I knew he was capable of it. But to see the capacity of what he can do. It shook me deeper than I thought it would." She paused. "When we talked though, and then afterwards, it helped. You know me. I want to know how things work. I don't like the unknown. Ten years of not knowing about Ian drove me insane. It doesn't change who Logan is, or how I feel about him. He confessed that he almost didn't do it. He feared showing that side of himself to me would make me afraid of him. I had to show him that wasn't the case."

Mestra chuckled slightly. "And so you took him to another cavern. I can understand that."

The shifting of the others in the small space alerted them. A quick breakfast followed in silence.

Mestra stood up. "We move as fast and for as long as we can. Logan, you and Cavon space yourself between the three of us. If we encounter anyone, they should be from Sanctuary."

"If they aren't?" Cavon asked.

"If they're not, get out of the way. Let us deal with it. No heroics. Leave the fighting to those trained for it." Martine spoke up, her voice firm.

Logan spoke. "We know our place, Martine. You won't see more of what happened last night unless there's no other way."

Arine studied Martine's face, waiting for her to believe Logan's words. It was one thing to know about magic; it was something else to see it done before your eyes.

Martine shrugged. "Good enough, I suppose."

They handed the two packs off to Logan and Cavon, since they weren't armed. Fighting without the extra weight would benefit them all.

* * *

The late afternoon sunlight filtered into the tunnel, letting them know the exit

124

wasn't far off. Mestra raised a hand, halting them. "We're not far off now. Let's go back to the last side cavern and rest. It's still a good way to Sanctuary, but I'd rather do it in daylight over dark if we can."

Arine spoke up. "Agreed." While she and Mestra knew the path well enough to go at night, the rest wouldn't. Martine had never been to Sanctuary, either. Resting now and moving at first light was the best plan possible.

She noticed Mestra hesitate as the rest moved through the narrow crevice. She paused, waiting.

"I'm going on tonight. Alone. I want to make sure they know we're coming, and what follows us. Cavon and Logan can't keep the pace I need to. And Martine…" Mestra whispered.

"You don't trust her," Arine stated.

"No, I don't. If I can speak with Mistress Bryn first, then we'll know if she truly is expected."

"And if your hunch is right?"

Mestra shrugged. "If I'm right, then you'll be met at some point with an escort home. She's come this far with us. Whatever her goal is, I'd give even money it's in Sanctuary. She's not going to hurt you or the boys before that happens." She placed a hand on Arine's shoulder, then moved with grace toward the meager daylight.

Arine moved through the slit in the rock to rejoin the others. Her mind raced to come up with a plausible reason why Mestra wouldn't follow.

Logan noticed first. "Mestra?"

Arine laughed. "You know how she is, Logan. Never can sit still if she's got the will to move. She's scouting ahead, making sure the trail's clear for the morning. Domine Elsa's still going to hunt for Cavon, marriage or no. Mestra's going to lead any lookouts on a merry little chase tonight."

She smiled, and dared a sidelong glance at Martine. The other woman's face was a studied mask, unreadable. Either she believed Arine, or she was calculating her next move.

Arine settled against the wall, legs stretched out across the opening. Just in case.

Cavon and Logan slept while she dozed. Martine was on watch, but Arine wasn't fully asleep. Mestra's concern echoed her own. There was something off with Martine. Outside of the familiarity between her and Sabine, they had no real evidence she was Moreja. And Talia found them somehow. It couldn't have been coincidence.

"Your friend doesn't trust me," Martine said, her voice low enough not to awake the boys but loud enough for Arine to understand her.

She gave up the pretense of sleep and straightened to a sitting position. "No, she doesn't. Would you, if the positions were reversed? A strange woman from a strange land claiming membership in the Sisterhood? Bearing a message for the head of our Order that's not written down?" Arine stared down the other woman. "Give me one good reason to believe you didn't betray us to Talia as a way for us to take you to Sanctuary."

Martine raised a single eyebrow. "If that was true, don't you also suspect me of slaughtering your brother and his family? Or handing them over to the Domines instead of making sure they were safely on the way back to the Far Lands?"

Arine didn't bother to hide the movement towards the dagger at her waist. "If any harm has come to Ian…"

"Not by my order, Arine. I was paid well to bring them here, and back home, safely. On the sea, a captain's word is law. None would dare disobey me, and I would never be allowed safe harbor at home if I harmed anyone on my ship."

The dark-skinned woman rose. Arine didn't hesitate, moving along with her. Slowly, the two circled the room.

"I've been left on watch, alone. I could've slit the throats of each one of you as you slept. When you and Logan slipped off, I could've killed Mestra and Cavon and ran ahead. Do you deny I've had opportunity?"

"No. The concern isn't for us. We know we'd be able to get back safely. You need us to get in. You don't know the way."

"So, what then? I'm sent to assassinate Mistress Bryn? Make sure the way's open for Talia and the army?"

"It's possible." The room was small, too small. If they were going to fight, the boys were going to get hurt before they were fully awake.

Arine watched, her dagger drawn, waiting. The next move was Martine's. Logan stirred on the ground behind the other woman, but Arine refused to change her focus.

Martine walked a few steps forward, to the center of the room. Deliberately, holding Arine's gaze, she knelt on the ground. The curved sword slid out of its sheath with a metallic hiss. "By all that my kind see as holy, I come as emissary to Mistress Bryn. To let her know her fight is ours. And to let her know an entire fleet of warships will be laying siege to Dawnbreak by now. It is time the Moreja came out of hiding, so that the men of the world will be given rights." She moved the sword so the point rested against the opening at the front of her tunic. "Should my words be false, I pray to the Mother of All, take my life now."

The vow, some of the same words used by Arine herself when she became Moreja, rang through her soul. She knew the weight of the words. And had seen the hand of the Goddess strike down those who spoke the words without truth behind them.

"Know that She will hold you to your vow," Arine softly spoke the end of the ritual. She waited as Martine rose and sheathed her weapon. The tension of the last few moments dissipated as the women faced each other again.

"Let's wake up the boys. Past time we got moving."

Chapter Fifteen

Arine didn't wait outside of Bryn's office for long this time. Mestra had already filled her in on their mission. The only thing she could really contribute was her discussion with Ian. And what happened with both Logan and Martine in the tunnels.

Bryn sat, calm as ever, behind her desk. "I'm sorry to hear Ian won't be joining us here. I know you've missed him a great deal."

"True, I have. I thought of him each time you sent one of the Sisterhood out on a mission, hoping he was the one they'd bring home. Still," Arine paused, "it's good to know he's happy. Taken care of. I can ask for nothing more for him."

Bryn nodded, "Good." Her tone told Arine the subject was closed. For Arine, as well as Bryn. There would be no more missions to convince him to return. His choice was made, and being honored. "We need to evacuate Sanctuary, and fast. I've already made the announcement. We're going to head through the tunnel behind the waterfall. It's wide enough on each side for us to pass. I've got emissaries heading to Recor. There's an abandoned keep, an old summer home of Sabine's, outside of town.

We'll be cramped, but it'll keep us safe until we can find a more permanent home."

"Why are we running, Bryn? Why not face the Domines, talk to them? We're not hurting anyone. We simply see things differently."

Bryn sighed, "In a perfect world, Arine, diplomacy would work. But this isn't one. The Domines are almost as corrupt as the male Kings of old, the ones who wanted to abuse magic. They rule through power and fear. Our time here was coming to a close, and I knew it. Between Talia's defection and magic coming back to men, it was only a matter of time before they'd march on us. They want to control that which they fear and don't understand. No amount of ink on parchment or signed treaties will erase that."

"Why march an army against us, though?"

"To prove they're right and we're wrong. That's it. We're different, accepting. It's in our nature to fear what we don't understand, be afraid of change."

She rose, and Arine followed suit. "Go. Be with Logan. Pack what you need. I have to speak with Martine now. We have precious little time, and can't waste it now."

* * *

131

The first wave of residents moved out the next morning. A group of Moreja accompanied them. It consisted mostly of families with young children, the elderly, and those who couldn't move fast. Those who could fight stayed behind, waiting, watching.

In truth, not many of them stayed. Less than twenty. Mistress Bryn refused most of the requests, telling them that guarding the rest was more valuable than staying behind. Arine had hoped she would send Logan away, but he remained. Mestra, Cavon, Martine…true fighters, yes. But not enough to do more than delay the inevitable.

Her eyes scanned the rough walls that had been their home for so long. Hollowed out from age and erosion, only the tunnel concealed by the waterfall connected back to the mainland. As isolated column of rock rising from the canyon floor, protecting them.

Arine tore her eyes from the retreating figures. The line was slowly disappearing. Less than an hour and it'd be down to the last of them. Waiting. Watching. Martine recommended that they wait until they saw Domine Elsa's army before they left. Give the illusion Sanctuary wasn't deserted. They all moved fast enough. They shouldn't be far behind.

Mestra approached, spyglass in hand. "I don't know how she did it."

Arine furrowed her brow. "Did what?"

Her friend didn't answer, simply held out the brass instrument and pointed towards a small crevice in the wall.

She moved towards the crack, fitting the large end of the glass into the opening. As she scanned the canyon below, she swore. Glinting in the late afternoon sun was the army bearing down on Sanctuary.

Their window for escape closed rapidly with every step that those troops took.

"How long?" She asked.

Mestra shrugged. "Not long enough. They're less than a day away. Camp tonight, attack tomorrow. That's what I'd do."

Arine looked up and caught the last few figures disappear into the waterfall's opening. Even if they had a full day, it wouldn't be enough. The moment Elsa or Talia entered Sanctuary the population was doomed.

"Logan wants to close the tunnel behind us, like he did near Dawnbreak. But we've got to distract them, fight them off longer. They're not going to move fast enough. We have to give them time."

133

"Let's go talk with Mistress Bryn. Maybe she's got some ideas to stall for time." Arine hoped more than believed that would be the case. The situation called for something drastic.

* * *

She sat on the edge, her feet dangling down the side of the tor. The first rays of dawn crept over her shoulder, making the vibrant colors lining the canyon dance. Even with the campfires of thousands of soldiers in front of her, she loved the way it looked. This was home. More so than her life had been with her mother. It was where she belonged.

She didn't turn her head as footsteps came up behind her. Logan settled next to her, a bit further from the edge. Smiling, she waited. He had never been fond of heights, even though he knew she loved to come here and think. He wouldn't have come up here if it wasn't important.

"How long, do you think?" His voice shattered the calm of the early morning.

Arine scanned the canyon below. "Not long. An hour, maybe two. Make sure you and the others are ready to go. You'll know when."

He nodded, "Soon as everyone's in the tunnel and behind me, I'll collapse it. Mistress Bryn wants me in there early, so there's no chance at me being injured beforehand. I'll do it, but I'd rather be with you. I won't leave without you."

"Yes, Logan. You will. You have to. If I don't make it in the tunnel, you do what you must. By then I'll be dead, and there's nothing you can do to save me anyway."

His face, transparent as always, showed his shock at her statement. "You talk like you don't expect to get out of here. Don't do that to me, Arine. Please. Don't leave me alone."

She smiled, trying to reassure him. "I'm not doing anything foolish, Logan. I want to live. But I want you to promise me you're not going to put your own life at risk because of something I choose to do."

"You're scaring me, Arine."

Leaning in, she kissed him tenderly. "Don't worry about it, Logan. For the first time, I'm finally certain what I have to do." She scooted back from the ledge before rising. "Let's go back with the others. We have to be ready before they wake up down there."

The first horn blew less than an hour later, a single note echoing throughout the canyon. Arine ignored it, her mind intent on the trip wire set up. Martine had brought with her some sort of black powder, swearing it would devastate the surrounding stone if set afire. Arine was skeptical, but Mistress Bryn had faith, calling it 'a countermeasure to be used only in cases of extreme emergency.' Their situation now certainly qualified. Following Martine's instructions, she and Mestra had rigged the various paths and buildings within Sanctuary with an elaborate network of wires. Each one led towards a small pile of the strange material. Trip the wire, and a burning candle tipped over, igniting it and triggering an explosion. Draw the troops in, make them give chase, and flee into the tunnel while Sanctuary broke apart and destroyed anything that was in the way. That was Bryn's plan.

Only Arine thought of a new one. If it worked, they'd be able to come back to Sanctuary.

So, she waited. To do this, she needed to be outside. Be where Talia and Elsa could see her. And, more importantly, the women fighting for them.

Her last trap set, she worked her way slowly toward one of the secret exits. There weren't many. Even among the Moreja, few knew them all. Arine had found this one by accident. Sliding between one of the last houses and the wall of rock, she found the crawlspace. The darkness enveloped her, but she didn't need light. One small bend up ahead and she'd have natural light to guide her.

The opening was big enough to stand in, but shielded from one side by an outcropping of rock. She chose her footing carefully, working her way around to the front of the tor. Where everyone in the army could see her. And hear her.

She waited, in full view of the troops. Talia wouldn't kill her without facing her first. She was predictable. There would be insults, challenges. All she had to do was wait.

A single rider moved through the ranks, making her way towards Arine. "Nice armor, Talia. It's not going to help you, but at least you'll die in something nice."

Talia reined her horse to a stop, "You're the one that'll die today, Arine. You and that monstrosity you claim to love. I think we'll kill your boy first, let you watch."

Arine straightened her back, standing tall. Her voice rang out. "Hear me, one and all. We are not your enemy. We only seek the right to live our lives in peace, live with the men we love. We do not fear magic, nor do we abuse it as was done in history. I recommend, if you want to live, that you head to high ground now."

Talia barked out a laugh, "High ground? Really? You got one of your boys planning on bringing the canyon down on us? You're a distraction, Arine. Worthless. More concerned with a boy than the world around you. Do you honestly think you can love him enough to keep him from doing magic without your permission?"

She smiled in return. "No. But I love him enough to make sure you never have the chance to abuse him." Arine closed her eyes, and found a peace inside her that she barely knew existed until now. She understood, more than ever, what Logan had said about magic being alive. Knew that it deemed her cause worthy, her sacrifice just.

The last thing she felt was the force of the water as it exploded from the rock behind her, flooding the canyon and pummeling her body against the rocks below.

Epilogue

"Logan! Over here!" Cavon called out to him. He turned his head, and located his friend standing near the edge of the water.

The front of the tor had exploded, allowing the water to spill from the pool and into the canyon. The rocky ledges around the new lake bore testament to the devastation of Arine's magic. Spears and swords lay next to bodies, all broken and battered. When the collapse had first occurred, he'd hoped Arine made it to safety. Two hours into the search, though, and his hope was fading.

Slowly, he made his way over towards Cavon. Mestra arrived before him, and moved a branch off of a body. It was Arine. Her face a peaceful mask, as if she slept. But he knew she was gone.

Kneeling, he let the tears flow. Gently, he brushed a strand of limp, wet hair away from her face. Her skin was cold, lifeless. One final kiss to her forehead in parting was all he could manage.

"She died so we may live, and will forever be remembered as the first woman to harness magic. Let us honor her." Martine's voice was low and filled with sorrow.

The four of them gently raised her body from the rocky shore and carried it back to Sanctuary.

The End

About the Author

Born in the late 60's, KateMarie has lived most of her life in the Pacific NW. While she's always been creative, she didn't turn towards writing until 2008. She found a love for the craft.

When she's not taking care of her family, KateMarie enjoys attending events for the Society for Creative Anachronism. The SCA has allowed her to combine both a creative nature and love of history. She currently resides with her family and two cats in what she likes to refer to as "Seattle Suburbia."

You can find KateMarie at the following sites:

Twitter: @DaughterHauk

FaceBook: http://www.facebook.com/pages/KateMarie-Collins/217255151699492

Her website: http://www.katemariecollins.com

Made in the
USA
Columbia, SC